Ulrich Haarbürste's Novel of

Plus Additional Stories

Ulrich Haarbürste

Dover Publications, Inc., Mineola, New York

Bibliographical Note

This Dover edition, first published in 2019 , is an unabridged republication
of the work originally printed by Serapion Books, Great Britain, in 2007.

Library of Congress Cataloging-in-Publication Data

Names: Haarbürste, Ulrich, author.
Title: Ulrich Haarbürste's novel of Roy Orbison in clingfilm : plus
    additional stories / Ulrich Haarbürste.
Other titles: Novel of Roy Orbison in clingfilm | Roy Orbison in clingfilm
Description: Mineola, New York : Dover Publications, Inc., 2019. | This
    Dover edition, first published in 2019, is an unabridged republication
    of the work originally printed by Serapion Books, Great Britain, in
    2007.
Identifiers: LCCN 2018053643| ISBN 9780486834672 | ISBN 0486834670
Subjects: LCSH: Orbison, Roy—Fiction.
Classification: LCC PR6108.A22 A6 2019 | DDC 823/.92—dc23
LC record available at https://lccn.loc.gov/2018053643

Manufactured in the United States by LSC Communications
83467001   2019
www.doverpublications.com

For Jetta

Contents

Roy Orbison in Clingfilm Stories

Roy in Clingfilm Story 1

It always starts the same way. I am in the garden airing my terrapin Jetta when he walks past my gate, that mysterious man in black.

"Hello, Roy," I say. "What are you doing in Düsseldorf?"

"Attending to certain matters," he replies.

"Ah," I say.

He appraises Jetta's lines with a keen eye. "That is a well-groomed terrapin," he says.

"Her name is Jetta," I say. "Perhaps you would like to come inside?"

"Very well," he says.

Roy Orbison walks inside my house and sits down on my couch. We talk urbanely of various issues of the day. Presently I say, "Perhaps you would like to see my clingfilm?"

"By all means." I cannot see his eyes through his trademark dark glasses and I have no idea if he is merely being polite or if he genuinely has an interest in clingfilm.

I bring it from the kitchen, all the rolls of it. "I have a surprising amount of clingfilm," I say with a nervous laugh. Roy merely nods.

"I estimate I must have nearly a kilometer in the kitchen alone."

"As much as that?" he says in surprise. "So."

"Mind you, people do not realize how much is on each roll. I bet that with a single roll alone I could wrap you up entirely."

Roy Orbison sits impassively like a monochrome Buddha. My palms are sweaty.

"I will take that bet," says Roy. "If you succeed I will give you tickets to my new concert. If you fail I will take Jetta, as a lesson to you not to speak boastfully."

I nod. "So then. If you will please to stand."

Roy stands. "Commence."

3

I start at the ankles and work up. I am like a spider binding him in my gossamer web. I do it tight with several layers. Soon Roy Orbison stands before me, completely wrapped in clingfilm. The pleasure is unexampled.

"You are completely wrapped in clingfilm," I say.

"You win the bet," says Roy, muffled. "Now unwrap me."

"Not for several hours."

"Ah."

I sit and admire my handiwork for a long time. So as not to make the ordeal unpleasant for him we make small talk on topical subjects, Roy somewhat muffled. At some point I must leave him to attend to Jetta's needs. When I return I find he has hopped out of my house, still wrapped in clingfilm. The loss leaves me broken and pitiful. He never calls me. He sends no tickets. The police come and reprimand me. Jetta is taken away, although I get her back after a complicated legal process.

There is only one thing that can console me. A certain dream, a certain vision . . .

It always starts the same way.

Roy in Clingfilm Story 2

In this fantasy I am driving along the Autobahn between Köln and Aachen.

A large Winnebago has pulled to the side of the road ahead. An anxious-looking man flags me down.

"This could be trouble," I say to Jetta. "It is certainly irregular." Jetta says nothing. Little do I know what is in store.

"Can you help me?" says the man. "I am Roy Orbison's tour manager."

"Also?" I say in polite surprise. I have already read the legend "Roy Orbison tour bus" on the side of the vehicle.

I get out of the car. "What seems to be the problem?"

He leads me to the back of the van. "Roy has succumbed to a heart attack and is clinically dead," he explains, indicating a certain well-known man in black sprawled on the floor of the vehicle.

"So," I say.

"Are you perchance a doctor?"

"No. I studied at a catering college for some years but was forced to leave for reasons I prefer not to disclose."

"*Ach!* Then I am at a loss what to do."

"There is one thing we might try," I say with elaborate nonchalance. "If we were to wrap him in clingfilm, this would prevent corruption setting in until we can get him to a hospital."

"It is certainly worth a try. But I have no clingfilm."

"Fortunately I have several rolls in the car." I go to the car and retrieve it. The tour manager looks anxiously over my shoulder as I set to work. "I must work undisturbed," I tell him. He nods and gives me privacy.

Now it is just me and Roy Orbison and the clingfilm. I start from the ankles and work up to the trademark dark glasses, wrapping slowly and carefully. Soon Roy Orbison is completely wrapped in clingfilm. He is like a big black beetle wrapped in a silvery cocoon. The satisfaction is unparalleled by anything in my previous existence.

"He is completely wrapped in clingfilm," I call to the manager. "I will accompany him as you drive to the hospital."

Four hours later Roy Orbison sits up in bed in the hospital and smiles at me.

"I hear I owe you my life," he says. "Please accept these concert tickets."

I bow politely. "There is something you perhaps should know. While you were in a coma I was forced to wrap you entirely in clingfilm."

"Quick thinking," says Roy.

"You did not mind?"

Roy's expression is unreadable. "I wasn't aware of it." But was there the slightest twinkle behind those dark glasses?

Of course, I reflect as I return to the patient Jetta, there can be no question of him enjoying it, for he was dead at the time.

Or was he . . . ?

Roy in Clingfilm Story 3

It begins innocently enough in the pet shop. I am seeking worms for Jetta.

"Hello there," says a vaulting tenor voice behind me. "We meet again."

I turn and take in the black clothes and trademark dark glasses. I bow and smile. "Mr. Roy Orbison, I presume. What brings you to our little emporium?"

"I was passing through town on my way to a rock star conference in Essen when I decided to get some deworming powder for my dog."

"Ah! How ironic! Your dog has worms and my Jetta eats worms." I decide to risk a little joke. "Perhaps we should bring the two of them together!"

But Roy does not laugh. The eyes behind the dark shades express no mirth. "What? What are you saying? Are you saying your terrapin should eat worms out of my dog's ass?" he snarls.

It is all going wrong. My palms sweat. I wish to die. I try to wake up.

I blush and mumble apologies. Fortunately just then a distraction arrives.

Two criminals burst in waving shotguns.

"This is a robbery!" they yell. "You two are hostages."

"Make them tie each other up," says the lead robber.

"*Ach!* I have forgotten the rope," says his cohort.

"I happen to have a roll of clingfilm with me," I offer diffidently. "Perhaps that would serve?"

"It will have to. Wrap that man in black in clingfilm at once or it will go badly with you."

"Very well." Trembling, I take out the clingfilm. "I am sorry, Roy, it looks like I have no choice."

"Do what you have to."

I start at the feet and work my way up. I wrap him as tenderly as a mother swaddling an infant. I marvel at the play of light on the miraculous translucence. Soon, Roy Orbison is entirely wrapped in clingfilm. I thank God that I was born to live this minute.

"He is completely wrapped up in clingfilm," I report.

"Good," says the bandit. "Now I want you to wrap the clingfilm around the two of you so that you are wrapped up with him."

My mouth dry, I stand pressed against Roy, who is wrapped completely in clingfilm. Awkwardly, I pass the film around both of our waists several times, until we are bound together by the miracle substance. My synapses overload with joy.

"We are both wrapped in clingfilm," I tell the robbers. "I am not completely wrapped, however, but there is more clingfilm in my briefcase if you would care to finish the job."

"No, that will do."

It certainly will!

It is an hour or more before the police come to release us.

"Well," I say to Roy Orbison, "it was nice to meet you again."

"I'm not a philosophical man," says Roy thoughtfully, "but it seems like we are bound together in some way."

"Yes—by clingfilm!" I say.

This time Roy does laugh.

Roy in Clingfilm Story 4

This time I am at the health spa having my cuticles attended to and procuring a pedicure for Jetta.

"Also," says the garrulous beautician as she works. "You will never guess. We are favored by a visit from a celebrity today."

"Unglaublich," I say without much interest. "Some dreary town councillor or rising star of the banking industry, no doubt," I say with a wink at Jetta.

"No, no," says the busybody as she plies her trade. "This is a big American rock star who wears iconic black clothing and trademark dark glasses. His name is Roy. . .Orbital? Orbheissen? Rasmussen? Something of that nature."

It takes a second or two for the penny to drop. "Black clothes and dark glasses you say. I implore you to think carefully. Could the man's name conceivably be Roy Orbison? This is a matter of extreme urgency to me."

"Yes! That was it exactly! Fancy, he is in the next room waiting for me to give him a seaweed wrap."

I rise from the chair. "I find I have to go out for a moment. You will please remain here and attend to Jetta. I have decided you will give her a shell wax. I will be locking the door after I leave to ensure your compliance."

"So."

"So."

I adjourn smartly to the next cubicle. Roy Orbison is lying on a massage table naked save for a strategically placed towel. Some soothing unguent has been applied to his face and slices of cucumber have been placed over his trademark dark glasses.

"Good day," I say. "Are you relaxed?"

"I am highly relaxed but expect to be more so following my seaweed wrap," says Roy.

"Regrettably I find we have run out of seaweed following a maritime disaster in which various contaminants were released destroying the world supply of sargasso for generations to come," I say smoothly. "Instead I urge you to try our new clingfilm wrap. The health-giving properties of this miracle substance cannot be overstated."

"Clingfilm?" Roy cannot see me but tries to peer round the cucumber slices occluding his glasses. "Don't I know your voice?"

"I am an eminent doctor and am to be trusted implicitly."

"Ah," says Roy. "Then you may commence."

"Speaking as a doctor, that is a wise decision."

I start from the feet and work my way up. It is strange for him to be naked as I wrap him but I suppose it would be too suspicious were I to ask him to put his trademark black clothes back on. I am like an Egyptian priest enshrouding his pharaoh. Soon, Roy Orbison is wrapped up in clingfilm. I let out a soft mew of content and mutely acknowledge that all things work for the best in this world.

"You are completely wrapped in clingfilm," I tell him. "To get the full benefits you must remain so for several hours or until someone comes and finds us. To keep you company I will stay in the room and breathe heavily."

"That is kind of you."

There follow several hours of almost unbearable bliss. Presently a masseuse comes and looks at us quizzically.

"We are closing now. Have you seen Frieda?"

"Yes, I locked her in the room next door."

"Ah. Why is that man in clingfilm?"

"Medical reasons."

"So."

I permit the woman to unwrap Roy as it is not in my nature to do so.

"You know," I say, "if you were to remain wrapped in clingfilm forever I estimate it could extend your lifespan by a thousand years."

"I will bear that in mind," says Roy.

And it wouldn't do my health any harm either, I almost add!

Roy in Clingfilm Story 5

Where does reality end and dream begin? Who can tell. . .

I sit before the television set absorbing the evening news with my terrapin Jetta.

"Also," says the news announcer, "tomorrow the famous conceptual artist Christo will visit Düsseldorf to wrap our statue of Prince Jan Wellem in a white sheet."

"How that man has wasted his life," I say. "To be obsessed with wrapping things in white sheets! What could be more pitiful?"

Jetta blinks slowly in agreement.

The announcer continues: "The famous rock star Mr. Roy Orbison, that well-known man in black, will preside over the installation of the new artwork."

"And yet," I say musingly, "who are we to judge? For which of us does not have his own private dreams he would like to act out? Even you, Jetta, in your secret terrapin heart may harbor dreams of wrapping certain things in other things. I believe I will attend Herr Christo's performance after all."

Jetta merely blinks again. Is there a hint of warning there?

Comes the morning, and various civic dignitaries and an interested crowd are gathered in the town square. Roy Orbison, laconic behind his trademark dark glasses, waits to unveil the statue of Jan Wellem so that Christo can then veil it again. I am at the forefront of the crowd with Jetta nestling in my coat and we have had a busy night. Little does anyone suspect what is about to befall.

The crowd grows impatient for the time for the installation has passed some minutes since. Murmurs of discontent at the inefficiency are heard and the hoi polloi look pointedly at their watches.

"I must speak to the mayor!" says a breathless flunkey.

"He may do so," says the mayor. "Let him approach me."

"I have to report that the conceptual artist known as Christo cannot be found! He has not been seen since the early hours of the morning when a man claiming to be delivering a terrapin visited his hotel room."

"Also!" The mayor is disconcerted. He eyes the unruly mob who are shuffling their feet and muttering slogans such as "Time waits for no man."

I cough diffidently and step forward. "Perhaps I may be allowed to take Christo's place? I have some small experience with wrapping things."

"Capital!" says the mayor. "Do so."

"But," says the flunkey, "the artist's large white sheets cannot be found either."

"*Ach!*" says the mayor. "This is a catalog of errors."

I cough again. "If you permit a suggestion. For sundry reasons I happen to have several rolls of clingfilm on my person. Perhaps they might suffice? Clingfilm is anyway a more appropriate material for a dynamic and modern city to wrap a statue in, is it not so?"

"You are a prudent and resourceful fellow. You will commence." The mayor takes the microphone. "I am pleased to announce that in place of the scheduled event Ulrich Haarbürste, a local man of commendable diligence, will now wrap our statue of Jan Wellem in clingfilm, a miracle substance befitting our dynamic city. Mr. Roy Orbison will now unveil the statue."

Roy starts to pull at a rope and then stops. "I think you should come see this, Mayor," he says grimly.

The dignitaries look behind the curtains and find that during the night the statue of Jan Wellem has been painted with various slogans denouncing the mayor. I whistle nonchalantly and pick a piece of lint off Jetta.

"Unglaublich," says the mayor. "This is a public relations disaster waiting to happen. The statue cannot be shown in such a condition."

"But the crowd!" says the aide. "If nothing is to be wrapped today they will tear us limb from limb."

"Then logically some substitute will have to be wrapped but I cannot think what."

"If I might make a suggestion," I offer. "It strikes me that we do not just have one landmark here today but also another—a pop cultural landmark." I bow to Roy.

"That is so. You will wrap Roy Orbison in clingfilm at once."

"If Roy does not object?"

"I do not object," says Roy. "Begin."

The mayor explains to the crowd that this bold experiment will put us at the forefront of conceptual art. There are interested mutters. My mouth is dry as I take out my clingfilm and begin to wrap Roy Orbison in it.

I wrap more carefully than ever before. Not merely personal gratification but civic pride is at stake. The sunlight glints on the translucent triumph of science. The faint rasp as I unspool it sends delirious brightly colored butterflies flocking through my stomach. I am like a tailor of the elves bedecking him in a shimmering suit of some magical material. Soon, Roy Orbison stands before all of Düsseldorf wrapped up in clingfilm. Silent white light floods my whole being and I become one with the universe.

"Fellow burghers!" I cry. "Behold! Roy Orbison is completely wrapped in clingfilm!"

The crowd cheers ecstatically. It is a moment of supreme triumph. I know how Alexander and Napoleon must have felt. I have conquered all. The whole world kneels before me. It is my will alone that has wrought this. I, Ulrich Haarbürste, am the king of kings. I am one with the godhead. Booming triumphant laughter wells up out of me and reverberates mightily about the square.

Suddenly the artist Christo appears flanked by policemen and points at me.

"That is the man! That is the one who seized me roughly and locked me in a cupboard."

"That is also the man I found loitering in the square last night with a pot of paint," says a policeman.

"This is very bad for you, you scoundrel," says the mayor.

"Uh-oh," I say to Jetta. "It is all going wrong."

The crowd turns ugly. They storm the podium with various cries.

"Seize him."

"Disarrange his clothing."

"Take away his terrapin."

"Confiscate his clingfilm."

"Banish him to a distant province."

I am manhandled roughly. I seek to explain myself but they will not listen. Roy is knocked off the podium and rolls around helplessly in his silvery straitjacket. My palms sweat. I wish to wake up. . .

I awake from my reverie and find myself back sitting in front of the television with Jetta. None of it happened after all but I have perhaps learned a lesson.

"Yes, Jetta, perhaps you are right. One should be careful which dreams one seeks to make real. . ."

And I switch off the television and we make off to bed.

But where does reality end and dream begin. . .

Who can tell?

Roy in Clingfilm in Space

(This tale was specially commissioned by the "Zoo Nation" science-fiction fanzine. Hitherto I have kept my tales of Roy in clingfilm strictly within the realms of plausibility but this scenario may be more fantastic than usual. Then again—who can say?—Ulli)

In this fantasy Roy Orbison and I are the pilots of a magnificent rocket ship powering through space.

"Adjust thrusters, Mr. Haarbürste," says Roy tersely, his calm capable hands adjusting the controls, the stars reflected in his trademark dark glasses.

"At once, mein Kapitan!" The precision-engineered BMW engines send us zooming through the stratosphere and push us back into our upholstered flight seats.

"Make your report, Lieutenant Jetta."

The screen wired to the pod where Jetta nestles snugly flickers into life. "WE ARE LEAVING EARTH'S ATMOSPHERE AND ON COURSE FOR SPACE" says the readout.

"So?" says Roy. "Capital."

The age-old problem of how to navigate the vast distances of deep space had been solved when it was discovered that terrapins had a unique ability to encompass the manifold plications of space and time. I and my terrapin Jetta immediately volunteered for an exploratory voyage. But who was to command this historic mission? The world was unanimous. There was only one man qualified to be mankind's ambassador to the stars: Roy Orbison, icon and enigma. Or as we must now call him, Captain Roy Orbison of the Space Pioneers.

Suddenly Jetta's translator flashes urgently: "LOOK OUT!"

It is too late. There is a metallic clang and the ship rocks violently.

Roy thumbs the communicator to Earth. "Düsseldorf, we have a problem," he says.

"We have been struck by an asteroid," I report. "One of the precision-engineered BMW engines has been knocked out of alignment. Unless it can be mended we will die."

"Suit me up," says Roy. "I'm going out there."

"Captain," I say nervously, "you are not going to like this. I am afraid we forgot to bring space suits on this mission."

"*Ach!*" says Roy. "This is a grave disappointment."

I clear my throat diffidently. "There is one thing we might try. As you know I had the foresight to bring many rolls of clingfilm with us for emergencies just such as this."

"I scoffed at the time but now I perceive you were wise. You will wrap me in clingfilm at once."

I retrieve some clingfilm from the Clingfilm Stowage Compartment where several hundred of the translucent rolls of joy glint softly in the cabin lights.

Roy Orbison unbuckles from his seat and floats out into the middle of the cabin, his black clothing billowing about him in the zero gravity like the folds of some black cloth manta ray. "Commence," he says.

As I set to work I seem to hear the strains of Strauss's "Blue Danube" waltz in my head. As I orbit him, weightless, it is as if we are performing some graceful ballet together. The clingfilm unfurls in languid arcs in the zero gravity and then girdles him gently as I spiral around him. Soon, Captain Roy Orbison of the Space Pioneers is completely wrapped in clingfilm. In all the infinite galaxies there is not a man as happy as I. Tears of wordless joy leak from my ducts and float off like little jewels, crystallized moments of ecstasy, tiny universes of rapture, perfect unto themselves.

"You are completely wrapped in clingfilm, Captain."

"Also. Let us see about this engine, then."

I tether him to me with a long umbilicus of clingfilm and Roy floats out of the airlock into space, protected by his airtight cocoon. Quickly he makes the necessary adjustments and we are saved.

"Emergency averted," says Roy on his return. "Now, helmsman, take us to the stars."

"Aye, aye, Captain!" I muse for a second. "Captain," I say, "the advanced civilizations we seek—what do you think they will be like?"

"I do not know," says Roy. "But one thing is for certain—they will know the value of clingfilm!"

And we laugh heartily and zoom off to infinity side by side.

But suddenly Jetta's screen comes to life again: "LOOK OUT—TIME WARP!"

Everything goes strange. It feels as though my internal organs are sucked out through my ears.

And then. . .

"I scoffed at the time but now I perceive you were wise. You will wrap me in clingfilm at once."

Roy unbuckles from his seat and floats out into the middle of the cabin. "Commence," he says.

We have gone back in time and I will have to wrap Roy all over again!

In space, no one can hear you squeak with pleasure.

Roy in Clingfilm at Christmas

In this heartwarming seasonal tale Roy is now my neighbor in Düsseldorf and often pops round to my house to borrow kitchen necessities.

It is Christmas Eve and Roy has popped round to enjoy a warming glass of Glühwein and help me affix tinsel to Jetta.

"*Ach*," says Roy suddenly, "I find I have forgotten to obtain a Christmas present for my mother, who is wintering at Baden."

I sip my Glühwein carefully and remark, "This will lead to familial tensions and unseasonal strife."

"It is so," says Roy.

"You know," I say thoughtfully, "it strikes me that the best gift a son can give his mother is himself."

"What you say has a certain validity yet how are we to dramatize this concept in such a way that my mother will not merely feel gypped out of a present?"

"Perhaps if we were to wrap you in Christmas wrapping paper and convey you to Baden."

"Also," says Roy, rising. "You will wrap me in Christmas wrapping paper and convey me to Baden at once."

"Regrettably I find we have run out of wrapping paper and the shops have now closed. Logically some substitute will have to be found."

"Yes, that is logical, but I cannot think what." Roy looks around the room seeking that in which he may be wrapped.

My mouth is dry. I tickle Jetta's paws idly and say, "You know, I believe I may have some clingfilm in the kitchen."

"Then the situation is saved. You will wrap me in clingfilm and have me stowed beneath my mother's Christmas tree."

I bow my assent and make to the kitchen. But when I open the cupboard I turn ashen and begin to quiver. For the cupboard is bare. The clingfilm has been used, all the rolls of it.

In alarm, I return to the living room and open the other clingfilm cupboards but it is the same story. I check the cache in my bedroom wardrobe and again there is none. I ransack the entire house from top to bottom. I look for the emergency rolls I keep hidden in the toilet cistern and inside lampshades. Everywhere there is the same horrible dearth of clingfilm. My palms sweat. I wish to die.

"Roy," I say, "I find I was mistaken. Due to an oversight I have no clingfilm in the house. I will not be able to wrap you in it. I am sorry, this has never happened before."

"Also," says Roy. "Perhaps some brown parcel paper?"

"I would rather die than wrap you in brown parcel paper." I am broken and pitiful.

And then it happens, the seasonal miracle. A cloud of soot billows from the fireplace and he comes down my chimney, that well-known man in red.

"Hello, Santa," I say. "What are you doing in Düsseldorf?"

"Attending to the distribution of presents," he says.

"Ah," I say.

"You have been good this year," he continues. "You have been orderly and polite and have kept your shoes neatly arranged."

I bow courteously. "Good behavior is its own reward."

"Nevertheless I intend to give you a present."

"May I inquire what?"

Santa Claus opens his sack, revealing dozens of silvery tubes. "It is many rolls of clingfilm."

"Capital," says Roy. "Now you may commence."

Trembling with anticipation, I take a roll from Santa's sack. I start at the feet and work my way up. I work with the craft and dexterity of an expert shopkeeper wrapping a purchase. Soon, Roy Orbison is completely wrapped in clingfilm. I am filled with peace on earth and goodwill to all men. As a seasonal touch I drape him with tinsel.

"He is completely wrapped in clingfilm," I say to Santa.

"Ho," says Santa, stroking his trademark white beard. "So this is how it is. Is it that you like to wrap him as a present to the world?"

"Who can plumb the mysteries of the human heart?"

"Who indeed? I confess to being envious of him. In my long life I have wrapped many gifts and yet, ironically, I have never been wrapped."

"Perhaps I might oblige? I have many rolls left."

"Commence," says Santa.

I start from his boots and work my way up. It takes a good half a roll to encompass his jolly round belly alone. Soon, Father Christmas is completely wrapped in clingfilm. It is not quite so good as wrapping Roy but it is enjoyable nonetheless and is certainly a feather in my cap.

"Both Father Christmas and Roy Orbison are completely wrapped in clingfilm," I say to Jetta.

I place Santa next to Roy and stand in between them. With some difficulty I wrap all three of us up together as best I can. We enjoy a quiet but satisfying yuletide until people from the social services come to release us.

God bless us one and all.

All Wrapped on the Western Front

(This was my entry for the EU–wide "Never Again" competition for a short story depicting the horrors of warfare. I did not win, alas. This tale takes place at Christmas too but its message is timeless.)

An icy wind blows across the fields of Flanders. It is December 24, 1917, and I am tending my trench and minding my own business.

My messenger terrapin, Jetta, comes crawling down the line with a dispatch from HQ gripped between her teeth.

"Attention," it says. "Beware of American attacks! If you see an American you must shoot to kill or bayonet them in the tummy. Be careful when affixing your bayonet or you may cut yourself."

I idly polish Jetta's spiked metal helmet and sadly ponder the horrors of war. It seems so impolite to have to bayonet people one has not been properly introduced to.

And on Christmas too! Dispiritedly I pull crackers with Jetta and present her with the warming woollen bootees I have knitted her but my heart is not in it.

I lean on the parapet and disconsolately sing:

> Stille Nacht
> Heilige Nacht. . .

And from across no-man's-land a vaulting tenor comes drifting:

> Silent Night
> Holy Night. . .

One of the foe is singing a carol!

"Hello," I call. "You have a nice voice."

"Thank you," calls the enemy. "I have been told I could turn professional."

"Perhaps you would like to see my trench?" I say.

"Very well," says the voice.

The man comes walking across no-man's-land treading gingerly for fear of landmines or worm-riddled corpses. I see he is wearing black clothing and dark glasses and has perhaps been on a mission to sidle up close to our trenches and eavesdrop on our chit-chat. Yet I feel no animosity, only a strange admiration.

He drops down beside me.

"My name is Roy," he says. "I am an American."

"Also?" I say with polite interest. "Mine is Ulrich, and this is my terrapin Jetta."

"She has a well-polished helmet."

I bow my acknowledgment.

"Your trench is remarkably free from rats."

"I try to keep it that way. I find it best to wrap the leftovers from our meals, snacks, and picnics in clingfilm."

"Clingfilm." Is it my imagination or does a manly tear escape from behind his dark glasses? "Then the Germans use clingfilm too. We are not so very different after all. The propagandists told us you wrapped things in inferior white grease-paper like savages."

Eagerly I say, "Perhaps you would like to see my clingfilm?"

"Very well."

"Due to wartime privations I have only managed to accumulate half a bunker full . . . "

Just then there is a high-pitched whistle and a bomb goes off in the trench. A bilious green smoke floods out and obscures everything.

"Gas!" I cry. Quickly I put on Jetta's gas mask and then fumble my way into my own.

"*Ach*," says Roy, "regrettably I find I have left my gas mask behind. Now my face will dissolve and my lungs turn to a bubbling pus. If I ever sing again I will sound like *guh, guh, guhhh*."

Diffidently I say, "I may be able to offer an alternative."

"I would embrace that alternative whatever it is," says Roy.

There is no time to lose. Quickly I run to the clingfilm bunker and return with a roll and commence to wrap him.

I start at his head and work my way down to his combat boots. It would feel more natural to do it the other way around but I must protect his face before it dissolves to a bubbling pus. I wrap him tightly and with military efficiency. Soon, Roy the strange American is completely wrapped in army-issue clingfilm. Within my heart desire and fulfillment conclude a lasting armistice.

"You are completely wrapped in clingfilm," I say. "Now you are safe from the ravages of the gas."

Roy makes a muffled sound that may be "I am glad."

Disaster has been averted and Roy has been saved. All too soon the gas disperses and I am forced to release him from his protecting cocoon.

"Thank you for your help," says Roy. "I must go now."

I bow. Shyly I say, "Perhaps I will see you on Easter, or Pancake Tuesday."

"I will provide the maple syrup," says Roy, "and . . . "

"Yes?"

"You bring the clingfilm."

And he walks off across no-man's-land taking a little piece of my heart with him.

The . . . end? Of warfare? But when . . .

When?

Roy in a Bubble

This time I am taking Jetta to be exhibited at the Düsseldorf Pet Show where it is my hope she will sweep all before her in the Miscellaneous Pets category.

Roy Orbison is to be the celebrity judge. This boosts my hopes as he has already shown himself a connoisseur of well-groomed terrapins and admired Jetta's lines.

However, when I meet him backstage before the show his eyes are unreadable behind his trademark dark glasses. "I will show no favor," he warns. "If Jetta is to take the prize rosette it will be on her own merits."

"I would expect nothing less," I say.

Just then there is a bark from where the various pets are massing. Roy gives a start.

"What was that?" he demands.

"A dog, perchance?"

"That was no dog . . . ," says Roy ominously.

Suddenly he gives a mighty sneeze.

"Gesundheit," I say.

But the sneezing is not all. Behind his trademark dark glasses his eyes are running and his face has become swollen and puffy and covered in red blotches.

"*Ach*," says Roy, "my allergies. Some fool must have brought seals here."

"Indeed, I believe there are a number of seals entered in the competition."

"Confound it! I loathe and detest those creatures for the fact is I am allergic to them."

"That is terrible, Roy."

"I do not wish to speak self-pityingly but all my life this tragic syndrome has set me apart and made me little better than half a man." He wrings his hands. "Whenever seals are to be part of an evening's entertainment I have to make my excuses and leave. My rock star friends are starting to think me a spoilsport and a poor stick."

"To be unable to go near seals! You must be the loneliest man in the world."

"It is so. More to the point, I cannot judge the contest in this condition!"

I scratch my ear and clear my throat.

"Roy," I say, "I believe I have an idea. Are you perchance familiar with the tale of the Boy in the Bubble?"

"What of it?"

I take out a roll of clingfilm and unravel it a little way with that sticky rasp that makes my tummy flutter with anticipation.

I say, "I happen to have a roll of clingfilm with me—"

"Capital," says Roy, interrupting me. "I perceive what is in your mind. Please go and garrote the seals with it at once."

I am taken aback somewhat and blink.

"Alas, Roy, an archaic bylaw dating from 1423 forbids the killing of seals at a public festival." This is a white lie as to the best of my knowledge there is no such foolish law. "I had in mind more—"

"Yes, I understand now. If you make me some gloves of clingfilm I can go and illegally bludgeon them to death without leaving fingerprints."

"But Roy, if you are seen—the negative publicity—"

Roy considers. "What you say is true, although it might boost my profile among disaffected and nihilistic teenagers from Düsseldorf's deprived lower-middle-class areas."

"I had the idea that—"

"Yes, I see. If you disguise my face with clingfilm I can kill the seals in anonymity."

"But your trademark black clothing would be recognized."

"In that case there is only one thing for it. You must completely wrap me in clingfilm at once!"

"I—but of course!"

I start from the ankles and work my way up. I must add several layers so that he may be disguised but I must wrap each limb individually so that he will be free to bludgeon the seals to death. Soon, Roy Orbison is completely wrapped in clingfilm. If I were a seal, I would clap my flippers and say "Arf."

"You are completely wrapped in clingfilm," I say.

"Now to massacre the seals," says Roy, picking up a length of lead piping.

"But Roy, perceive—you are no longer swollen and sneezing!"

"*Ach* so," says Roy. "It is true. This miracle substance is protecting me from the seal pollen. For the first time in my life I am a whole man!"

Just then a little seal comes lolloping up to us, its wet nose glistening.

Gingerly Roy pats it and it rubs its nose against him.

"I never knew how beautiful they were."

He spends the rest of the day frolicking with the seals, rolling around on the floor with them and tickling them. Instead of bludgeoning them with the lead pipe he throws it for them to fetch.

Regrettably he awards the prize rosette to a seal. Jetta comes second and is sulky and withdrawn for a week.

However, the main thing is I enabled Roy to have a new experience and wrapped him in clingfilm again.

Shrink Wrap

In this story I am earning a living going round offering primal scream therapy door-to-door.

I decide to start at Roy Orbison's house as he is a rock star and so will be at home during the day.

I step smartly to his door and ring his doorbell.

"Good afternoon," says Roy, opening the door. "How may I help you?"

"I am going round offering primal scream therapy door-to-door," I explain. "Would it be convenient for me to come in and extol the benefits?"

"It would," says Roy. "I was about to embark on some hoovering but the need is not pressing. You may enter."

Roy shows me into his living room. I set down my primal scream practitioner's bag and my assistant Jetta and launch into my sales routine.

"In primal scream therapy the subject achieves catharsis by regressing to early childhood and emitting a mighty scream," I say.

"That sounds admirable," says Roy. "I am always keen on self-improvement. Let us proceed."

I nod. "So then. If you will imagine you are a young child."

"I am doing so," says Roy.

"Capital. Now if you will commence to scream."

"Argh," says Roy.

"*Hmm*." I stroke my chin.

"I feel no better," he complains.

I muse for a moment. "Perhaps if we were to regress you further and reenact the primal birth trauma itself," I suggest.

"By all means," says Roy. "If a thing is worth doing it is worth doing thoroughly."

"One idea occurs," I say. "I happened to bring a roll of clingfilm with me in case of emergencies. How would it be if I was to wrap you in it so as to enact a return to the womb?"

"I see no objection," says Roy. "Commence to do so."

"Then if you will assume a fetal position."

Roy curls up on the floor in a fetal manner. I start at his tucked-in feet and work my way around. I wrap tenderly and reverently. Soon, Roy Orbison is enveloped in a magnificent amniotic membrane of clingfilm. My very nostrils tingle with glee.

"You are completely enwombed in clingfilm," I say.

"Capital," says Roy, somewhat muffled.

"For the therapy to work you must remain like that for nine months."

"Also?" says Roy, surprised.

"So as not to make the ordeal unpleasant for you I will keep you under a giant maternity dress I happen to have with me. I will stroke you and croon to you and feed you through an umbilicus made of clingfilm. If you require anything, just kick."

For the first time in our acquaintance Roy looks somewhat alarmed. Even his trademark dark glasses cannot dissemble his concern at this turn of events.

"I am expecting my manager at five o'clock," he says.

"I will send him away," I say. "I will send everyone away. A fetus cannot sing!"

Roy looks distinctly nervous.

"But my career?"

"You are too small to have a career, my little budding blossom. When you are born and grown up you may, although banking is a much steadier line of work."

Roy fights his way out of the clingfilm and screams, an ear-splitting window-rattling vaulting tenor shriek of terror.

"There," I say, "isn't that better?"

"Very much so," admits Roy. "I feel a man reborn. How much do I owe you?"

"I will give you a concessionary price of five euros. And," I say with a merry twinkle, "that does not include the delivery charge!"

"Please go away now," says Roy.

South Sea Pirates

(This is another alternative world, or a somewhat-less-plausible-than-usual story. I make no apology. That is what the imagination is for and if there is at least a psychological truth then art may result.)

In this one Roy and I are merry pirates of olden times plying our trade across the South Seas on a magnificent sailing ship.

We also have a concession to sell clingfilm to any uncivilized natives we may find.

"Yo-ho-ho, Mr. Haarbürste," says Roy merrily, swinging jauntily from the rigging. He wears a trademark black eyepatch over each eye.

"Yo-ho-ho and a bottle of schnapps, Captain!" I reply equally merrily. "What a fine day to be a pirate and roving clingfilm salesman!"

"Indeed."

Suddenly a bell is rung from the terrapin's nest at the top of the mast, where Jetta is keeping lookout.

"Land ahoy!" I say. Merrily.

"Perhaps they will have some booty we can plunder! Gold deutsche marks, or index-linked bonds for preference."

"Or we may at least be able to open up a new territory for the sale of clingfilm."

"Yes, having already cornered the Tasmanian market we would be salesmen of the month."

We launch a boat and with several of our crew row to the uncharted island, polishing our cutlasses and jaunty pirate boots so as to make a good impression.

Little do we suspect what is about to befall. . .

We land on the beach and romp intrepidly through the jungle, encouraging ourselves with merry pirate songs and cries of "Yo-ho-ho."

Then we come to a village of savage islanders! They are very scary and are covered all over in barbaric tattoos that say things like "Mother" and "LUFC." They are armed with many spears so we put away our cutlasses and present our business credentials.

"Good day," I say.

"Good day," says the chief of the savages. "I hope you are well."

"I am very well, thank you. We come to bring you the benefits of civilization. We are here to sell you clingfilm!"

I open my sample case and they gasp! They examine the rolls wide-eyed.

"Shiny yet translucent!" they say. "Supple and yet clinging! You may demonstrate the benefits of this miracle substance to us by and by."

I am conducted to a place of honor.

"However," says the chief, "we do not do business on an empty stomach. First we must eat."

"By all means," I say.

"You shall be the guest of honor at our banquet."

"Nothing would please me more! There is nothing I like better than a simple repast of South Sea island pineapples and breadfruit."

"That is unfortunate," says the chief, "for we are Polynesian cannibals and we are going to eat your crew!"

"Also," says Captain Roy, not so merrily. The crew also look rather dismayed at this plan but they are surrounded by spears before anyone can object.

"So then. If you will please to enter the cooking pot."

Roy raises one of his trademark double eyepatches for a second so as to see where he is going as he steps gingerly into the pot. Lamentably his jaunty pirate boots will now be full of water. The crew are prodded in after him and a fire is lit.

When the water is simmering they commence to take the crew out of the pot and kill and eat them one by one. They fall to with great appetite and there is many a cry of "Yum" and "Tasty." So as not to be impolite I pick idly at the cabin boy's ear and fill up on the salad.

Soon, Captain Roy is the only one left in the pot. . .

However, before they get to him they are finished. With a burp one discards the bosun's arm.

"I am full," he says.

"I too, I could not eat another morsel," says a second.

"It is agreed," says their chief, "the meal has concluded. Now to dispose of the leftovers. Throw them off the cliff in the usual way."

Quickly I say, "But gentlemen, why throw away the leftovers when they can be kept fresh for another day?"

"What is this you say? It is not possible!"

"If you permit, I will demonstrate! I will wrap your leftovers in clingfilm and I guarantee they will remain fresh for a week."

"I will test that claim," says the chief. "If the clingfilm does keep our leftovers fresh, we will order a gross and fill your ship with breadfruit, daughters, and interesting stones. If it fails we will remove your kneecaps and lightly braise them in a jellyfish sauce, as a lesson to you not to indulge in empty hucksterism."

I bow and take out the clingfilm.

"I am sorry, Roy," I say, "it seems you are leftovers and must therefore be wrapped."

"I confess to some hurt at being eaten last," says Roy, sloshing from the pot. "I fancied myself far more appetizing than the midshipman."

I start from the jaunty pirate boots and work my way up. I wrap tightly and carefully so as to preserve all his succulent freshness. Soon, Roy Orbison is completely wrapped in clingfilm. My heart makes landfall on the Island of Dreams.

"He is completely wrapped in clingfilm," I report.

Less eagerly I also wrap the arm of the bosun and cover a bowl of coleslaw.

"Capital," says the savage. "Now to embark on the taste test."

Roy is rudely stowed in a larder-hut for a week, completely wrapped in clingfilm. So as not to make the ordeal unpleasant I accompany him, sitting as closely as I can and stroking his shimmery loveliness consolingly when he is not conscious.

The week passes in an eyeblink and all too soon we are hauled out to undergo the freshness challenge. Barbarically they tear the clingfilm from Roy and the other leftovers without any ado and commence to sample.

"Unglaublich!" exclaims the island's leading food critic, chomping on the bosun. "The coleslaw is perhaps on the turn but the bosun's arm is as fresh as ever! Thanks to this translucent miracle of civilization we need never go hungry outside the tourist season again."

"Then if you will please to free us?" I say.

"I will not do so!" says the chieftain. "I confess to some peckishness and am very glad that Captain Roy retains his succulent freshness, for I am now going to eat him!"

However, just then Jetta drops out of a tree onto his head, knocking him unconscious. A rescue party from the ship bursts out of the jungle armed to the teeth. The savages drop their spears and we conclude a treaty which gives us exclusive rights to supply them with clingfilm for the next ten years.

"All is well that ends well," says Roy. "Now to fill in a satisfying uptick on the sales chart."

"Of course," I say roguishly, "by rights we should take you back to the ship in a doggy bag!"

"Someone else is as fresh as ever," comments Roy.

"It's a Wrap"

In this one we are visiting a film set in the Düsseldorf film studios.

Roy is seeking to branch out into a film career. From small acorns grow mighty squirrels, and he is starting out auditioning for a tiny part as a Roman soldier in a Hollywood studio's remake of *Caesar and Cleopatra*.

In addition I have applied feathers and a cardboard bill to Jetta so that she may test for the role of Cleopatra's duck.

That also is not a large part but any exposure may be valuable at this stage of her career.

Alas, no sooner have we arrived than a studio flunkey gives us bad news.

"The duck is out, it is now a terrapin."

I curse the random malice of fate that has scuppered Jetta's chances of stardom. However, I decide to stick around and see if any good can yet be salvaged from the situation.

The director is preparing to audition for the role of Cleopatra.

"I want my Cleopatra to be mysterious and enigmatic," he says. "Her eyes should be unreadable at all times."

An idea occurs. Discreetly I cough to attract his attention and incline my head toward where Roy is standing.

The director's mouth hangs open and the hotdog he is about to put into it slips forgotten from his grasp.

"Stop!" he yells. "Stop everything! Cancel the auditions! Send Julia Roberts and Estelle Getty back to the coast! You there!" he yells at Roy. "What is your name?"

"Orbison," says Roy shyly, "Roy Orbison."

"That'll never work on the marquee. We'll change it to Alluria Schlupfwinkel." Roy bridles somewhat at this. "No, don't move!" yells the director. "Don't move!"

33

Roy remains still. The director paces around him making strange framing gestures with his hands.

"Put your hand on your hip and say, 'How do you do, Caesar, so you're the guy they named the salad after,'" he instructs Roy.

Roy does and says this.

"Gentlemen!" the director yells. "I have found my Cleopatra! Put fake breasts on that man in black at once!"

Roy is mounted with fake breasts and exotic blue eyeshadow is applied to the upper portion of his trademark dark glasses.

"We will go straight to scene one!" cries the director. "This is a dynamite scene. Caesar has just conquered Egypt and Cleopatra has herself delivered to him rolled up in a fancy carpet and is then unrolled provocatively at his feet."

Nervously a flunkey bows and says, "Due to industrial action in the carpet-weaving sector we have been unable to obtain a carpet for this scene."

"You are fired!" screams the director, who is American. "You are all fired. You will never eat sauerkraut in this town again."

Diffidently I cough and say, "If I may be permitted to offer a suggestion. For sundry reasons I happen to have with me a roll of clingfilm, an exotic substance far more fitting to a Queen of the Orient than any moth-worn piece of carpet. Indeed, I have sometimes contemplated replacing the carpets in my own house with it. It strikes me that rolling Cleopatra up in clingfilm instead of a carpet might bring just that surprising twist required to give this timeworn scene new life."

"What a shit idea, assbandit," says the director, who is American. "You are fired! Clear out your locker and throw yourself down the commissary steps. I have a much better idea. We will use clingfilm instead of a carpet! You there!" He points at me and I bow. "Wrap that man in black with fake breasts in an exotic carpet of clingfilm at once and a golden future in this industry awaits you, kiddo."

"If Roy does not object?"

"If it will further my film career I do not object."

It is strange to be wrapping him while he wears fake breasts. Indeed I have noted before that it is hard to wrap breasts in clingfilm as they protrude in unsightly ways. This was one of the factors that led to my unfortunate divorce—that and the fact that the woman was not interested in wearing. . .a certain costume.

Nonetheless I work diligently and with a craftsmanship befitting a Technicolor cinematic epic. Soon, Roy Orbison is completely rolled up in a carpet of clingfilm. In the final edit of my life this will go on the highlight reel.

"He is completely carpeted in clingfilm," I announce.

"Action!" cries the director. "Unroll the carpet!"

Unfortunately the men playing Cleopatra's servants tug the clingfilm carpet to unroll too vigorously and Roy rolls out so far and fast he knocks Caesar over and then rolls off the stage.

"Cut," screams the director. "Take it again from the top."

"You mean," I say, my spine tingling, "we have to do it all over again?"

"What are you, goddam slow? We'll do it over and over until it's perfect! Why, I have often done so many as a hundred takes for a single scene."

And so it goes. All in all I am forced to wrap and unroll Roy so many as seventy-eight times.

All too soon, however, the shot is in the can.

"This is a crap scene anyway," says the director rudely. "I think I will cut it and put in something with motorbikes. You are all fired, especially Cleopatra."

"I do not like the film industry," says Roy, rubbing his various bruises. "In future I will stick to music."

"In truth," I say, "I cannot see you in a film."

Except, I think to myself, one certain special kind of film. . .

(I mean clingfilm.)

The
Roy Orbison
in Clingfilm
Novel

Chapter 1

It starts at the concert that Roy Orbison is playing in Düsseldorf. I am in a privileged position in the front row with my terrapin Jetta after having been gifted with free tickets for sundry reasons explained in my previous tales.

Roy has executed various songs of his repertoire with commendable diligence.

"Thank you and good night, Düsseldorf," he says as he prepares to take his leave. "You have been a well-behaved audience." He gives me a special nod and I nudge Jetta and bow to acknowledge the compliment.

"Please give us more," implores a voice.

"He may have a tram to catch," I remonstrate.

"I had not thought of that," admits the voice.

"Time is not pressing," says Roy. "It is somewhat irregular but even though I have finished my usual set I will perform another song or two at no extra cost."

"Capital," says the crowd. There are mutters of approval at his work ethic and zeal.

Roy adjusts his dark glasses and prepares to regale us with his trademark vaulting tenor.

But then disaster strikes!

"*Ach*," says Roy, glancing upwards. "It has started to rain. It looks as though I will not be able to perform any more after all."

"This is a disappointment," says a voice from the crowd. "He has trifled with us and cruelly dashed our expectations."

"You are a fraud, Mr. Orbison," calls another. "You have lost touch with your fan base." There are murmurs of discontent.

"What can he do?" I remonstrate. "No man can contend with the random malice of the elements. With all the electric rock instruments bedecking the stage he runs the risk of electrocution or similar mishap should he attempt to perform in the rain."

But the many-headed monster that is the crowd is not to be appeased. To my horror a slice of orange peel is tossed onto the stage, fortunately missing Roy but grazing his amplifier. There are various cries.

"Seize him."

"Storm the stage."

"Rend his trademark dark clothing."

"Dangle him upside down until we are given a refund."

"Show this American rock dandy how we arrange things in Düsseldorf."

I nestle Jetta closer to my bosom, for an emotional tinderbox such as this is no place for a terrapin.

Meanwhile Roy looks from the growling crowd to the trickling rain to the electrical sonic equipment which is even now starting to spark and crackle ominously.

"It looks as though I am trapped between a rock and a hard place," he comments wryly. "It seems as if I have no choice but to perform no matter the peril."

But if Roy touches his instruments he will surely be electrocuted! But if he does not do so—who knows what extremity the crowd will resort to in their displeasure?

How is this to be resolved? You may find out in chapter two. Little do you suspect what is about to befall. . .

Chapter 2

Hello, and welcome to chapter two. If you recall at the end of the last chapter Roy was in an awkward predicament between an unruly crowd on one hand and the almost certain risk of electrocution or humiliating wetness on the other.

How, I asked, was this to be resolved. . .?

Read on and all will be revealed.

Who could have foretold that I, Ulrich Haarbürste (accompanied by my terrapin Jetta), would find myself clambering onto the stage occupied by Mr. Roy Orbison, that well-known man in black? Nevertheless such is the case.

"Forgive me for intruding, Roy," I say with a diffident cough. "But it occurs to me that I may be able to offer a way out of your predicament."

"I cannot possibly imagine how," says Roy.

"If you permit, it seems to me that what is required here is some sort of covering to protect you from the ravages of the rain."

"It is so," says Roy. "But where such a covering is to be procured is beyond my wit to ascertain."

"If I might suggest—by some fluke of Dame Fortune it falls out that I am carrying a roll of clingfilm in my jacket. Perhaps that might suffice?"

"It will have to," says Roy. "You will cover me in clingfilm at once. Hurry for we can have only minutes before the disenchanted crowd rushes the stage and perpetrates some unpleasant harm upon me."

"Very well," I say.

I start from the ankles and work my way up. I work quickly and efficiently as though I had been rehearsing this moment all my life and had procured black-suited mannequins on which to practice. Soon, Roy Orbison is completely wrapped in clingfilm. I almost purr with the unbridled delight.

"You are completely wrapped in clingfilm," I report.

"Capital," says Roy. "Now you will see some rock and roll."

Roy hops close to his microphone and resumes his rock minstrelsy, somewhat muffled by his clingfilm coating. By the end of the second song the crowd are won over and hang their heads in shame at their earlier impoliteness. The disaster has been averted!

"I owe you my life," says Roy as he hops offstage. "At the very least I believe they would have scuffed my shoes. Give this man and his terrapin backstage passes," he instructs a roadie.

I bow my thanks and attach Jetta's pass to her paw as Roy is released from his filmy cocoon by the roadie.

"Boss," says the roadie, "I have to report that a reporter from *Rolling Stone* magazine is outside hoping to interview you."

"*Ach*," says Roy. "Am I to have no rest after my concert? I cannot openly offend these arbiters of rock star status and yet I wish there was some disguise I could adopt in order to leave without him accosting me."

"*Hmm*," I say. "It is certainly a predicament." I decide to risk a puckish observation. "You know, it strikes me there is a certain irony here. Any other man in such a situation would perhaps resort to wearing dark glasses in order to disguise himself. And yet in your case it is impossible, for wearing your trademark dark glasses it is impossible to mistake you for anyone else!"

Roy thinks about this impassively for several seconds and then begins to laugh. "It is so," he says ruefully. "It is impossible to mistake me for anyone else . . . "

Little do we suspect that a terrible irony lurks in that very remark . . .

Why is it so? And how is Roy to evade the importunities of the rock press?

Aha! You may not know at this point. But if you proceed to the next chapter you are likely to find out.

Chapter 3

Now the story continues.

You may remember that at the end of the last installment Roy was perplexed as to how to avoid the untimely attentions of the rock press without being impolite. The possibility of some sort of disguise had been mooted.

If you do not remember this you should certainly reread the preceding chapter to refresh your mind.

And so at this exciting juncture we resume.

Gratifyingly Roy is still laughing at my little joke. "My dark glasses are of no use," he says again. "It is so, it is so."

I cough diffidently and open my mouth to give forth: "Of course, there is one thing we might. . ."

But I am rudely interrupted by the loitering roadie, attempting to join in with the mirth.

"Perhaps if Mr. Orbison were to *remove* his trademark dark glasses *that* would make a good disguise!"

My palms sweat. It is all going wrong. Once again my attempts at urbane comedy have backfired on me. The thought of Roy without his trademark dark glasses is too awful to contemplate.

In my alarm and confusion I am regrettably short with the man and snap, "Such a thing is unheard of and I do not recall anyone canvassing your opinion. Go and fetch some complimentary backstage worms for my terrapin at once."

The luckless underling bows his assent and makes off.

"To everything its season," says Roy. "Enough mirth and tom-foolery for now. Let us put our minds to the problem of how I am to slip by the stage-door jackals of the press without causing offense."

"You know," I say, "it strikes me as somewhat unfortunate that you were released from your clingfilm wrapping so speedily. While clingfilm is remarkable for its miraculous transparency, in the event of a really, really thick wrapping with many, many layers, there is a cumulative effect of opacity so that in the end whatever is wrapped becomes an impressionistic blur embedded at the heart of a silvery cocoon in the most delightful way."

"Also?" says Roy. "There is more to clingfilm than one would at first suspect. In my rock star lifestyle I have not had time to go into this matter."

"I on the other hand have devoted some time to experiments in this line, purely in an amateur way," I admit modestly.

"What I fail to see is how this connects to our current predicament," says Roy.

"Listen and you shall hear of my plan," I say.

"Proceed to expound it," says Roy.

"I will do so," I say.

But just as I open my mouth to vent my suggestion the presumptuous roadie reappears in a state of great excitement.

"Mr. Orbison," he says, "I have to report that I have found a false beard left behind by a previous performer. Surely this will solve your disguise problems!"

What will happen now? Will the roadie's ridiculous beard scheme take precedence over my own more interesting and plausible plan? And what on earth can my own plan possibly be anyway?

You must wait patiently until the next chapter for enlightenment. . .

Chapter 4

Here we are at chapter four. I am becoming increasingly impatient at the need to recap what has gone before for the benefit of those who may have forgotten in the interim.

Certainly I hope no one is so foolish as to read the chapters one after the other without pause, for thereby you will deprive yourself of the joys of anticipation and wondering what can happen next.

However, if you leave it too long between installments you may forget the previous developments. I estimate that a week is a good length of time for you to mull over the ramifications of each chapter and tease yourself with speculations as to how the situation can possibly be resolved. If you intend to leave it longer than that, it may be wise to take notes about the contents of the foregoing chapter to refer to when you resume, for in future I do not intend to provide this service as it is slowing down the action.

Also. If you recall Roy and myself were debating how best to provide camouflage to enable him to avoid the loitering hounds of fame and thus be spared the need to provide his opinion on topical matters of the day.

A garrulous roadie had uninvitedly gate-crashed our deliberations in order to propound a foolish scheme involving Roy donning a false beard.

I, on the other hand, had hinted at the existence of a mysterious plan, the nature of which I had not yet divulged. . .

Whose scheme will prevail? Read on and your curiosity will not go unsatisfied.

I stare in annoyance at the false beard with which the optimistic flunkey believes Roy may conceal himself.

"*Hmm*," I say, thinking quickly. "Good work, my fellow." And I seize the beard and put it on myself. "This will indeed be adequate to disguise me. Now, where is the disguise for Mr. Orbison?"

"But—"

"What? You do not have one? A pretty kettle of fish! You had best scurry off and procure one, had you not?"

The man stammers incoherently and then clicks his heels and leaves.

"You cannot get the staff," says Roy.

"The poor man is in out of his depth," I say, stroking my false beard happily. "Now. In the event he should be unsuccessful, perhaps I should propound my own scheme at fuller length."

"You should do so," says Roy. "I confess my curiosity is whetted."

"Like all great ideas it is simplicity itself. It occurs to me—"

But at that instant I am again interrupted by the overeager roadman!

"Mr. Orbison!" he cries. "Our problems may be over! I have found an Elektra mask left over from a production of Sophocles at this venue!"

"An Elektra mask," I say, again thinking quickly. "Well done, my fellow. That will certainly suffice to disguise my terrapin Jetta." And I take the mask from him and put it on Jetta, whom it indeed renders unrecognizable, as she has never acted in Greek tragedy. "Now, where is Mr. Orbison's disguise, or did you overlook that again?"

"But—"

"May I suggest you depart and do not return until you have fulfilled your mission?"

The unfortunate man retires in confusion.

"He has outlived his efficiency and should be pensioned off," says Roy. "Also. About this plan of yours."

"I intend to wrap you in a great deal of clingfilm and wheel you past the reporter on a trolley," I say very quickly.

"A capital idea," says Roy. "Commence."

"Very well," I say.

I take the roll of clingfilm, which has already seen service once this evening, from my jacket.

I start at the feet and work my way up—

And stop at the shin!

For there is no more clingfilm on the roll! With a sickly rasp the last of it flies off the tube and adheres to the bottom of Roy's trademark dark trousers poignantly, fluttering limply like the flag of a defeated army, a banner of doomed dreams.

"Uh-oh," I say to Jetta, "it is all going wrong."

Jetta looks back at me mutely, her face a mask of woe . . .

TO BE CONTINUED (in chapter five).

Chapter 5

This is chapter five. Without wishing to speak boastfully I believe that chapter four was very good, in particular the dramatic ending.

However, it will soon become apparent that I have played a narrative trick on you. In my defense, however, this was purely for your heightened enjoyment as you will soon perceive. If when all the facts are laid before you, you have any complaints about this matter we can take it up another time, provided you remain calm and pleasant in any communication with me.

So then. If we cast our minds back to the previous happenings we see that chapter four concludes in a cliff-hanging situation. It looks very much as though I will not be able to wrap Roy in clingfilm for there is no more clingfilm left on the roll! It ends poignantly with me looking in alarm at Jetta, her face a tragic mask.

Chapter five resumes the action immediately following these events.

"Roy," I say, "I regret to announce there is no more clingfilm left on this roll."

"This puts a crimp in our plans," says Roy.

"Yes it would," I say, "were it not for the happy circumstance that, as chance would have it, I happen to have at least one other roll of clingfilm about my person, and possibly more than that. Not a suspicious number, but perhaps a somewhat surprising number when compared to the statistical average."

"Also?" says Roy. "This is fortuitous. Therefore there should only be a slight delay in the wrapping as you change to a new roll. Resume when it is convenient."

"I will do so."

I put the empty tube back in my pocket, for something so redolent of fond memories should not be discarded carelessly, if indeed ever. Then I extract a new roll of clingfilm from the inner regions of my clothing, pausing a moment to admire it in all its strong yet supple and transparent loveliness. As ever, I take a second to marvel that it is still entirely legal. Sometimes I wake in the night with a sudden fear that someone may come to confiscate my clingfilm and I run to count it and clutch it and think of new hiding places. But then I remember that they may not do so and I go back to my pillow with a happy smile on my face.

But with Roy about to be wrapped in clingfilm this is certainly no time for a digression!

I start at the ankles and work my way up. As the object is to efface Roy's various trademark features and render him unrecognizable in a silvery chrysalis under many, many layers of clingfilm, I work industriously and with a tireless zeal. I circle around him repeatedly like some clingfilm-trailing celestial body orbiting some impassive black planet. Before too long, Roy Orbison is completely wrapped in clingfilm to a depth of many, many layers. The joy cannot be measured on any scale of values yet invented.

"You are completely wrapped in clingfilm to a depth of many, many layers," I say.

"Capital," says Roy, very muffled.

I step back to admire my handiwork. Roy resembles some Stone Age rock god perfectly preserved within a clingfilm glacier. His outlines are satisfactorily blurred by the cumulative refractions of the deceptively transparent miracle of polymerization.

I decide to test the disguise on the much put-upon roadie, who just then comes running back crying, "Mr. Orbison! I have to report I have found a pantomime horse costume! Perhaps that . . . "

I hold my breath and wait.

" . . . But where is Mr. Orbison?" the unwitting flunkey asks open-mouthed. "All I perceive is some kind of glinting plastic monolith with a dark six-foot shadow at its center in the place where he used to stand!"

I repress a chuckle and seem to hear Roy, do the same, although it is very hard to tell beneath the several cubic feet of clingfilm encompassing him. Jetta paws at her Elektra mask as though she is unable to vent her mirth while wearing it, although perhaps she merely wishes to be free of it in any event.

The roadie paces all around Roy, scratching his head in puzzlement. Finally I let him in on the secret.

"That *is* Mr. Roy Orbison!" I say.

"Unglaublich," says the man. "This must be some uncanny kind of magic!"

"No, my fellow," I say. "Or at least—only the magic of clingfilm!"

From within the clingfilm megalith I seem to hear a vaulting tenor chuckle.

So it is proven that our disguise is able to deceive a humble roadie.

But will it suffice to get him past the vigilance of the waiting rock journalist . . . ?

For that, my friends, you will just have to wait to find out . . .

Chapter 6

You may recall that at the end of the last chapter I had satisfactorily tested Roy's clingfilm disguise on the unsuspecting roadie.

Now, read on to discover whether it will work on the rock journalist waiting to importune Roy with various tiresome questions about plectrums and crowd safety and so forth.

"Fetch a trolley," Roy's muffled voice orders the roadie, for this time he is wrapped in clingfilm to such a depth he would be unable to even hop or shimmy.

"I will do so," replies the roadie.

He does so.

We load the Roy/Clingfilm monolith onto the trolley and push him toward the exit where the *Rolling Stone* journalist is waiting vigilantly. Seeing that everyone else is in disguise, even my terrapin Jetta, the roadie feels left out and dons the head of the pantomime horse.

"There is nothing to see here," I say as we wheel Roy past the loitering hack.

"Hold a second please," says the journalist, perhaps scenting a story.

"Yes?" I say politely.

"I was hoping to have a word with Mr. Roy Orbison, that well-known man in black, in order to canvass his opinion on sundry matters of import to our readers."

"Also?" I say attentively, thoughtfully stroking my false beard. Next to me the horse-headed roadie bridles nervously but I keep cool and Jetta is impassive behind her Elektra mask. "I wish you luck finding him," I say courteously.

"May I inquire what you are pushing on the trolley?"

I think quickly. "An entirely unremarkable and nondescript man-sized mass of clingfilm we are taking to be measured out of reasons of curiosity," I say smoothly.

"Also," says the journalist. "I confess to being curious about that large mass of clingfilm myself. It seems to me I see certain shadows lurking in its depths which, while not immediately recognizable, nonetheless strike me as indefinably familiar."

"So?" I say. "But then, without wishing to cast aspersions, you are a rock journalist and as such have doubtless damaged your brain with a series of late nights and poorly lit concerts."

"It is true," says the man sadly. "I do not remember the time when I was last in bed at a reasonable hour and my brain is no longer to be relied upon."

I say, "I do not blame you, for zeal in your chosen profession almost requires such a lifestyle. But the taxation on your strength may perhaps lead you into mental error. Furthermore clingfilm can be a very deceptive substance; therein lies its eternal mystery. I may say that, although I keep regular hours, I have at times seen unusual apparitions in clingfilm myself when I have studied it for long enough."

"I will detain you no longer," says the man.

"Good luck with your lonely vigil," I say.

We bow and wheel Roy out into the street and the overhelpful roadie all too soon releases him from his clingfilmy carapace.

"Our stratagem succeeded at all points," says Roy. "Now my way is clear to make a getaway. Return the trolley to where you found it and tidy up after us," he instructs the attentive roadman. "Strike the stage and have it forwarded to our next destination. Our gypsy rock caravan next convenes at Aachen."

"Your instructions will be obeyed." He departs.

"Now," says Roy. "I have a show business party to attend. As you have been of inestimable service to me tonight perhaps you and Jetta would like to join me."

"We should be delighted!"

"So. Accompany me down this street."

I start to accompany Roy down the street but after several steps he stops suddenly with a look of dismay!

"*Ach*," says Roy. "This is a source of disappointment. I failed to remember that the party is to be a fancy dress party and I neglected to obtain a costume. We will not be able to attend after all."

Now what can take place! You do not know. But if you wait for the next chapter you will find out. In this matter you are but puppets on my string.

Chapter 7

In the surprising climax of the last chapter an unfortunate situation had arisen wherein Roy looked unable to attend a show business party due to a regrettable lack of a costume.

Is he in fact doomed to be excluded from the gathering of his entertainment peers. . .? Read on and all will be made plain.

First I must assure you that I have not forgotten that in chapter two I remarked that a terrible irony was concealed in Roy's statement that it was impossible to mistake him for anyone else. You have been waiting patiently to find out why this was, but the time to tell you is not yet. As a novelist I must keep many pots on the boil and I cannot attend to everything at once. But you will be given the relevant information when it becomes needful to know and in the meantime the protracted suspense is part of the enjoyment.

So. Now with chapter seven.

"I am sorry to have cruelly dashed your hopes," says Roy, forlorn. "But we cannot attend a costume party without costumes or we will be shamed for our lack of zeal. I for one will not brook this."

"Nor I," I say. I tickle Jetta's nose thoughtfully. "And yet . . . perhaps there is a way we can still attend."

"I fail to see it," says Roy. "Even your notably fertile resourcefulness is not equal to this problem, my friend."

"At least allow me to try," I implore. "After all, perhaps there is some answer so simple it is staring us in the face." Idly I finger a certain cylindrical object in an inner pocket. "Perhaps there is some way we could . . . improvise costumes, from everyday substances near at hand."

"Improvising will not suffice," says Roy. "Not just any costume will do. Rivalry is fierce in rock circles and if I am to make a splash at the party my outfit must be both witty and eye-catching."

"*Hmm*," I say. "Plainly this will require some thought."

"Think away but I am at a loss as to what you can possibly come up with."

I stroke my false beard and pontificate.

"Let us take it in logical steps and perhaps we will manage to arrive at a solution," I say. "To be witty your dress must be something appropriate and yet with a surprising twist, is it not so?"

"It is so," says Roy.

"Also. What would be appropriate to you? What are your remarkable features? One thing occurs to me. You are an Emperor of Rock Music, are you not?"

"I do not wish to speak boastfully," says Roy.

"Then I will do so for you! You are an Emperor of Rock. So. Perhaps your costume should be something appropriate to an emperor."

"Your logic is tortuous and yet I cannot deny it has a certain validity," says Roy.

"So. What else does one think about in connection with you? I will tell you one thing: your dark clothing. It is something of a trademark with you, is it not?"

"It would be foolish to deny it."

"In fact, you never wear anything else, is that not the case?"

"That is the case," Roy concedes.

"Very good," I say. "Also. What could be more surprising than for you to come to the party in some new clothes?"

"Very little," says Roy. "It would be an occasion for comment and some good-natured raillery."

"So. What we must try to think of is a costume that says 'Emperor' and yet also says 'New clothes,' must we not?"

"It appears we must," says Roy.

"Then with this in mind let us brainstorm and endeavor to think of such an outfit."

"Perhaps if I was to dress as Napoleon and yet wear a brightly colored Rasta beanie in place of his trademark bicorne hat," says Roy.

"A capital idea," I say uneasily. "Yet how are we to obtain a Napoleon costume, to say nothing of a Rasta beanie?"

"*Ach*," says Roy. "That is a drawback."

I place a finger on my lips and hum thoughtfully.

"You know," I say at length, "I believe I have the glimmerings of an idea. . ."

What can my idea be? You would venture almost anything to find out but I will not tell you until the next chapter.

Chapter 8

In this chapter you will find out whether Roy is to attend his show business party and what costume he can possibly wear.

At first glance it would appear that it is impossible to find a costume, but such is not the case . . .

"Tell me, Roy," I say, "are you familiar with the famous tale of the Emperor's New Clothes, in which an emperor is completely garbed in a splendid outfit made out of a perfectly transparent material?"

"Heaven!" says Roy. "I am assuredly familiar with it and a costume based on this fable would meet the case perfectly, being both provocative and subtly self-mocking. Yet how are we to convey this concept in such a way that it will not merely be mistaken for indecent exposure?"

"Perhaps," I venture, "if we were to garb you in a material which is completely transparent and yet not quite invisible as it has the property of catching fugitive twinkles of light in the most mischievous way?"

"That would meet the case perfectly, and yet I do not believe such a miracle substance as you describe can possibly exist."

I cough diffidently and withdraw a roll of clingfilm from my clingfilm pocket. "With all due respect, Roy—I beg to differ."

"*Ach* so!" says Roy. "Then the way is plain. You will garb me in a splendid outfit of clingfilm at once."

I nod my assent. "As you wish."

With trembling hands I locate the end of the roll and prepare to begin. But a difficulty arises.

"Should I not first remove my black clothing?" says Roy.

The thought of Roy without his trademark black clothing makes me somewhat uneasy and confused. "I do not believe that will be necessary," I say. "Even worn over your normal clothes the splendid outfit of clingfilm will be sufficient to create the impression we wish to convey."

"Very well," says Roy. "You may commence."

I start at the ankles and work my way up. I am like some gentleman's outfitter privileged to work with the most gossamer-light fabric yet invented. I must wrap each limb individually and with a minimum of layers so as to obtain the effect of a set of splendid transparent robes. In this instance I may not wrap his head but I fashion a wonderful crown of clingfilm and set it atop him. As a final touch I contrive a flowing clingfilm cape such as some happy emperor of a clingfilm-based kingdom might be attired in and affix it to his shoulders. Soon, Roy Orbison is completely garbed in clingfilm. I sink to my knees with rapture and stare wonderingly at my own fingers in stunned disbelief at the magic that is within them.

"You are completely garbed in clingfilm," I tell him.

"Capital," says Roy. "Now we may go. My only fear is that someone else at the party may have hit upon the same costume."

Will someone else be wearing the same costume or will Roy be the belle of the ball? Fiend that I am, I shall force you to await the next chapter to find out!

Chapter 9

Previously in this saga it has been related how I contrived a splendid costume of clingfilm for Roy that he might wipe the eye of his show business rivals at the fancy dress party. But the fulcrum of suspense was, would anyone else have hit upon the same costume?

Read on and the answer will not elude you.

Quickly I attend to costumes for myself and Jetta. I remove the Elektra mask from Jetta and place my false beard on her back, so that she will resemble some shaggy Ice Age proto-terrapin of the Pleistocene era. For myself I retrieve the pantomime horse head from where the roadie discarded it and insert the empty clingfilm tube into its neck and secure it there with a few deft twists of clingfilm so that it in effect becomes a hobby horse. Clutching this as if riding it, I place the Elektra mask on the top of my head so as to act as a makeshift riding hat. It is my hope that I will thus resemble Elizabeth Taylor in *National Velvet*.

Roy is at first unsure of this. "I perceive that Jetta is some shaggy throwback to the time of glaciers, but may I inquire what your costume is?" he says.

"I am Elizabeth Taylor in *National Velvet*," I say.

"Also," says Roy. The trademark dark glasses study me for some time. "The resemblance is not exact but it works on an impressionistic level," he concludes.

"If need be I will say 'Whoa' and 'Giddy up' to reinforce the effect," I say.

"Capital," says Roy. "I believe we will make a splash. My one admonition is that if Elizabeth Taylor should happen to be at the party you must pretend to be Tatum O'Neal in *International Velvet*."

"I will do so."

"Then let us make to the party."

I follow Roy along several streets to the house where the party is. Roy gives a final adjustment to his splendid clingfilm regalia and rings the doorbell.

Appropriately enough the door is answered by Jim Morrison out of the Doors. The irony does not escape me but I decide not to risk remarking upon it at this stage.

"Welcome to the party," says Jim Morrison. "You may enter."

We wipe our feet and enter the house.

"So," says Jim Morrison looking Roy up and down. "The Emperor's New Clothes. I wish I had thought of that and confess to some envy."

"Eat your liver out, Morrison," says Roy.

"I admit myself bested," says Jim Morrison.

"It is all thanks to my tailor," says Roy magnanimously, "and a certain substance that has proved its usefulness on more than one occasion tonight . . . "

Jim Morrison regards myself and Jetta. "And here we have some sort of groovy hippy terrapin and Tatum O'Neal in *International Velvet*."

"That is close enough," I say generously. I perceive that Morrison is wearing a buckskin loincloth and a feather in his hair. "May I say I admire your Pocahontas costume?" I add.

"I am an Indian shaman," says Jim Morrison briefly.

We follow him into the living room. There I see Yul Brynner, that well-known actor with no hair, sitting on a couch next to Mitzi Klavierstuhl, the sprightly weathergirl from *Guten Abend Düsseldorf*, Jetta's favorite celebrity. They are trading urbane small talk and show business gossip but at our entrance Yul Brynner rises courteously and says, "Welcome to my party."

"Hello, Yul," I say. "What are you doing in Düsseldorf?"

"Filming a further installment in the Magnificent Seven saga," he replies. "Certain sections of old Düsseldorf have a borderline resemblance to a nineteenth-century Texan cattle town."

"Also?" I say. "I had not noted it."

"It is not so striking," Yul Brynner admits. "Frankly my location scout may have outlived his efficiency."

Yul has his arms folded and is wearing oriental pants. He is either reprising his role from *The King and I* or dressed as Jeannie from *I Dream of Jeannie*. After the debacle with Jim Morrison's costume I decide not to venture a compliment but instead to keep my ears open for any clues which may be dropped.

Yul Brynner meanwhile has no hesitation in admiring our outfits and proves to have a keen eye. "The Emperor's New Clothes," he says. "Congratulations, Roy, a triumph of the costumier's art. It is a capital drollery which works on several different levels. And here we have . . . some sort of shaggy Ice Age proto-terrapin of the Pleistocene era, I believe. And Roy, I had not known you were dating Elizabeth Taylor!"

I hesitate for a moment, fearing perhaps my costume may be too good and will lead to scandalous rumor, but then Roy chuckles and so do I.

Yul Brynner says, "May I introduce you to Mitzi Klavierstuhl, the effervescent weathergirl of *Guten Abend Düsseldorf* and a platonic friend of mine?"

"We have met before," says Roy, bowing. "There are few strangers in the world of show business."

Mitzi Klavierstuhl says, "Roy, I apologize for failing to predict the unexpected rainstorm which menaced the finale of your concert. I hope the performance was not interrupted."

Roy bows to me and says, "I was able to escape wetness thanks to the offices of my good friend Ulrich Haarbürste, a local man of commendable diligence whom I now have the honor to introduce to you."

I bow to Mitzi Klavierstuhl. "You probably hear this all the time," I say, "but my terrapin perks up whenever you appear on the screen."

Mitzi Klavierstuhl smiles graciously and says, "Thank you, and please write to our advertisers and tell them the same thing."

"I will do so," I say. "May I present her?"

"By all means."

"Her name is Jetta."

I present Jetta to Mitzi Klavierstuhl, who says, "You are to be complimented on your terrapin-grooming skills. On *Guten Abend Düsseldorf* we are confronted with many splendid animals but your terrapin is of a prize-winning caliber. May I hold her?"

"She would be delighted!" I pass Jetta to Mitzi Klavierstuhl, who makes the kind of soft cooing noises people tend to make who do not realize you may talk to terrapins quite ordinarily. Jetta looks frankly starstruck for a second as Mitzi Klavierstuhl holds her, her head protruding all the way out of her carapace in a way that usually indicates she wishes to look at something closely, then recovers her dignity somewhat and affects nonchalance.

Yul Brynner claps his hands and says, "To everything its season. Enough urbane small talk for now. Let us sit comfortably and the party may commence!"

This chapter has now gone on for some time and you may be tired out so I will call a break. It is somewhat irregular to end without a cliff-hanger but until the next chapter you may content yourselves with speculating on what the show business party will be like. . .

Chapter 10

Without any ado I will commence chapter ten. It is usual and polite to have a certain amount of preamble before resuming the action but in this case I will dispense with it as there was no cliff-hanger last time.

If you recall Yul Brynner had just ordered that everyone should sit comfortably so that the party could commence in an orderly fashion.

And may I say, I hope that you too are seated comfortably, dear reader! For this is necessary if your attention is not to wane. I do not advocate a slovenly posture, as this may lead to problems in later life, but a certain degree of comfort will certainly enhance the experience.

Also. I will now resume.

"So," says Yul Brynner when we are all sitting comfortably, "now the party may begin."

He claps his hands and flunkeys come in from the kitchen bearing all manner of party foods, which they place on the table.

"Let us commence to eat, drink and be merry," says Yul Brynner. "You will find there are all manner of good party foods provided: caviar, vol-au-vents, peanuts, custard, jelly, trifle, cucumber sandwiches and cocktail sticks with cubes of cheese upon them. Do not stint yourselves for the supplies are virtually limitless. Various beverages are available on request."

With murmurs of gratitude at his largesse we commence to sample the manifold delights.

"But hold!" cries Yul, smacking his trademark bald head. "I am neglecting your terrapin Jetta!" He claps his hands again to summon a flunkey. "Fetch a bowl of prime Pomeranian worms at once," he orders.

"Prime Pomeranian worms!" I gasp. "That is manna from heaven for a terrapin."

Yul folds his arms and smiles. "Only the best for the guests at my party."

"Yul Brynner is renowned throughout the show business world for the hospitality of his table," says Jim Morrison, somewhat muffled by a mouthful of jelly.

The flunkey returns with a bowl of prime Pomeranian worms and Yul points out to whom they are to be delivered. Jetta blinks slowly in astonishment and then falls to with great gusto.

"Now," says Yul Brynner, consulting a clipboard, "the next item on the agenda is the awarding of prizes for the fancy dress competition."

I hold my breath in anticipation. Jim Morrison puts down his jelly and leans forward eagerly. Roy's eyes are unreadable behind his dark glasses but Mitzi Klavierstuhl, who carries a large hammer and is either Thor the Weather God or Martin Luther preparing to nail his theses to the door of the church in Wittenberg, looks studiedly nonchalant.

"After due deliberation," says Yul Brynner, "I have decided to award the prizes as follows. . ."

I am tempted to make you await the next chapter to find out but it would be naked cruelty to do so, so I shall refrain.

"The first prize goes to Roy for the Emperor's New Clothes! The second prize is awarded to Jetta the terrapin for her hairy Pleistocene throwback costume. Mitzi comes third for Thor the Weather God. Honorable mention goes to Ulrich Haarbürste for most creative use of a horse's head."

Roy seems gratified while Jim Morrison hisses with chagrin. As for myself, honorable mention is not bad considering I threw the costume together at the last minute. Flunkeys cough politely and present us with small inscribed trophies.

"May I now discard my costume?" asks Mitzi Klavierstuhl. "This hammer is somewhat heavy."

"By all means," says Yul Brynner.

"However, I shall feel out of things being the only one uncostumed."

"I shall accompany you," says Roy gallantly, and somewhat to my regret removes his splendid costume, leaving him once more sadly bereft of clingfilm.

"Now we are very relaxed indeed," says Yul Brynner. "I believe it is time for some party games."

"Musical chairs," urges Jim Morrison.

"Musical statues," suggests Roy.

"Grease-the-piggy-sideways," says Mitzi Klavierstuhl.

"We may come to such sports in the fullness of time," says Yul Brynner. "To my mind there is only one way to launch a successful party, and that is with a game of pass-the-parcel. I confess to being a fiend for it. It is a capital diversion which works on several different levels."

"It is so," says Roy. "There is nothing quite so certain to break the ice and make a party go with a swing."

"Then it is agreed," says Yul. "We will start with pass-the-parcel. Therefore, Roy, I will ask you to hand me the parcel I instructed you to prepare and we may commence."

Roy is mute and unmoving.

Yul says, "Did you not hear me, Roy? I asked you to hand me the parcel I told you to bring."

Roy says, "Regrettably I find I neglected to bring such a parcel."

A silence falls. My palms sweat on Roy's behalf.

"*Ach*," says Yul Brynner, "this is a grave disappointment. . ."

Will the party be ruined by Roy's mistake? Or is there some way this mischance can be turned into an unexpected source of joy?

No man can read the future. But you, fortunate reader, can wait to read the next chapter!

Chapter 11

At the end of the last chapter it was revealed that Roy had omitted to bring a parcel to pass in pass-the-parcel.

There is a silence in the room save for the minute sounds of Jetta steadily working her way through the prime Pomeranian worms. The fate of the party is undoubtedly in jeopardy.

Or . . . is it? Read on and you shall see.

I cough discreetly and say, "If you permit me, Roy, it is naughty of you to tease Yul in that way. We have assuredly brought a pass-the-parcel parcel and have left it in the front hall." I do not dare to wink but try to convey through my tone that I have something up my sleeve. Or as it happens, in an inner pocket . . . (Although, come to think of it, I do also have a certain something up my sleeve, for emergencies.)

". . . That is so," says Roy uncertainly.

"Also!" says Yul Brynner. "I am man enough to accept a little teasing and I confess that the relief I am experiencing now the truth has been revealed is not unpleasurable."

"But hold," says Jim Morrison, frowning, "I saw no parcel in the front hall."

I say, "With all due respect, Jim, you are a self-destructive Dionysian figure and as such have doubtless corroded your brain with a sequence of deferred bedtimes and shamanistic frenzies."

"It is so," says Jim Morrison sadly. "I have felt somewhat out of things since the early 1970s. I am able to see into mystic realms but my brain is not to be relied upon for ordinary purposes of verification."

"Then if you will permit, Yul, we will now retrieve the parcel."

"You may do so," says Yul Brynner. "And hurry, for if I do not unwrap something soon I will not be answerable for the consequences."

Roy and I rise and bow and make to the front hall.

"I have proved myself a bungler," says Roy. "My lack of diligence has been a source of shame and discredit."

"You have had much on your mind tonight, Roy."

"Nonetheless my lapses have brought me to the brink of humiliating social disaster," says Roy. "Thank heaven for your quick wits. I perceived your plan in a flash."

"You did?" I say, surprised.

"Indeed," says Roy. "Our course is clear. We will flee the party and banish ourselves to a distant province. Perhaps we may enlist in the French Foreign Legion and attempt to find redemption under the harsh desert sun. We will be forced to abandon Jetta but Yul is too honorable a man to punish her for our failings."

"Also," I say carefully. "That is certainly a possibility. But what if I could present an alternative to an ignominious exile?"

"I would certainly seize on it," says Roy. "I admit it would grieve me never to see the cleanly boulevards of Düsseldorf again."

"Then may I relate my plan?"

"Proceed to expound it," says Roy, "but I confess to some scepticism that the situation can be retrieved. If Yul is not given a parcel to unwrap his wrath will be implacable. I would rather endure a lifetime beneath the savage suns of Africa sampling the redundant complexities of French cuisine than feel the whiplash of his scorn."

"Then," I say, "we must give him a parcel to unwrap!"

"I am at a loss as to what you can possibly have in mind," says Roy. "For one thing we have no newspaper and if we venture out in search of some we will be forced to ring the doorbell to gain readmittance, thus rendering our subterfuge transparent to even the meanest intellect. Furthermore, we are without sticky tape."

"If I may make so bold, Roy, there are other substances besides newspaper which are very, very good for wrapping things in," I say, "and one in particular I can think of which has the miraculous property of staying wrapped around something without need of any sticky tape whatsoever . . ."

I withdraw a roll of clingfilm from my inner pocket with a flourish.

"*Ach* so," says Roy, "I begin to see the light. But hold! What can we possibly wrap in this miracle substance to serve as the prize?"

"That," I say, "will require some thought . . ."

What will be the outcome of my thought? That is for me to know and you to wring your hands over until the next installment . . .

Chapter 12

Cast your minds back and you will see that at the end of the last chapter Roy and I had decided to improvise a pass-the-parcel parcel out of clingfilm.

But, what could possibly be interred in this parcel in order to serve as a prize? Continue to read and before many minutes have passed you will be much the wiser.

"Come," I say, "let us put our heads together."

"By all means," says Roy.

"You know," I say, "the lack of a conventional prize to be wrapped may work to our advantage. Instead, perhaps we could wrap some completely surprising item the revelation of which would make this the best party ever and you the undisputed Mr. Fun of the entertainment kingdom."

"At present that title is held by Johannes Doppelzimmer, the puckish arts-and-crafts correspondent of *Guten Abend Düsseldorf*," says Roy. "I confess I would love to steal his crown."

"Doppelzimmer, pfui," I say disparagingly. "You are ten times the madcap."

"He has a deft way with the use of joy buzzers," says Roy doubtfully.

"You leave it to me and once word of this party gets round Doppelzimmer's antics will seem as stale as yesterday's leftovers in the dark days before the invention of clingfilm," I promise. I knit my brows thoughtfully for some seconds. "I have it! What if *you* were to be wrapped in the parcel, and, at a climactic moment, burst forth from the last piece of wrapping and shout, 'Surprise!'?"

Roy is silent a moment. "You are the greatest gagman since Chaplin," he says at last. "No party should be planned without retaining you as a consultant in matters of tomfoolery and mirth.

Such a prank would be talked about long after we have gone down to dust. The way is clear. You will wrap me in a pass-the-parcel parcel of clingfilm and convey me to the living room at once."

I bow. "As you wish, Roy."

"Commence," says Roy.

I start from the ankles and work my way up. This situation calls for unusual demands of my art and yet could be my greatest triumph to date. I work thoughtfully and with diligent attention to results but still with an almost unbearable ecstasy coursing through my veins. In this case there must be many layers, but the clingfilm must be broken from the roll in smallish lengths before being applied to Roy, so that when the parcel is unwrapped each person is allowed to remove an interesting amount and yet the enigma of the contents is left intact for several rounds. Nevertheless, before too long Roy Orbison is completely wrapped in clingfilm. Celestial choirs seem to burst forth and give vent to their joy.

"You are completely wrapped in clingfilm," I announce.

But then something strikes me.

". . . Apart from your feet!" I add.

This will never do. If Roy's shoes are to remain unwrapped then it will not really be a parcel and there will certainly be little mystery as to the contents. I point this out to Roy and he gives vent to a muffled exclamation that sounds like "*ach.*"

I think quickly. "The way is plain," I say. "I must lay you horizontally on the floor so as to be able to obtain access to your feet."

There is a muffled noise that sounds like "Commence." I gently lower Roy to the floor and set to work again.

I start at the ankles and work my way down. I cannot help noting and approving how immaculately kept his shoes are. I work breathlessly but competently, not even omitting the soles of his shoes. Soon, Roy Orbison is completely wrapped in clingfilm, even his feet. My eyes roll round in my head and I start to babble and prophesy in several regional dialects.

"You are completely wrapped in clingfilm," I say, "even your feet."

"Capital," says the muffled Roy.

With some difficulty I pick up the parcelled Roy and carry him into the living room.

How will the unusual parcel be received? Aha, but you must sit upon your curiosity until the next chapter.

Chapter 13

Those who remember chapter twelve will recall that I had wrapped Roy in a pass-the-parcel parcel of clingfilm so that the party might go with a swing. For my part, I might add, it has already accomplished this purpose.

I return to the living room carrying Roy horizontally.

"My word," says Yul Brynner, "that is a parcel of the most magnificence. But why has Roy been so remiss as to allow you to carry it on your own? And why does he now remain in the front hall instead of rejoining our circle of gaiety?"

"Regrettably while we were fetching the parcel Roy was struck down with an unspecified ailment of a nature not likely to be life-threatening but likely to impair his social functioning and joie de vivre," I say smoothly. "He has gone home, shutting the door quietly, and conveys his apologies."

"*Ach*," says Yul, folding his arms, "I am displeased at this turn of events. I call Roy a jibber and a poor stick for these actions. By his deeds he has placed the success of the whole party in jeopardy. I knew I should have invited Johannes Doppelzimmer in his stead."

"Doppelzimmer, there is a man," concurs Jim Morrison.

"He is a deft hand at grease-the-piggy-sideways," says Mitzi, "and he has raised the palming of joy buzzers to the level of an art form."

"Decidedly we should have invited Doppelzimmer."

From within the parcel I seem to hear a vaulting tenor snigger. Little do they suspect . . .

"In fairness to Roy," says Yul Brynner, brightening, "I must say that he has wrought a pass-the-parcel parcel of almost Babylonian splendor. I cannot wait to get at it."

"Perhaps on the other hand," I suggest diffidently, "we should leave it inviolate until the very end of the party so as not to risk anticlimax?"

"*Pah*," says Yul, folding his arms again and pouting, "that is a foolish idea. Who can concentrate on jelly or grease-the-piggy-sideways when there is a fine big parcel to be unwrapped? Let us have at it before I burst with the tension."

He claps his hands and flunkeys bring a record player into the room. As I have no interest in unwrapping Roy I volunteer to work the music and Yul does not object.

I reflect thoughtfully that life is very strange and no man can fathom the mysteries of human nature. Some people, like Yul, like to unwrap things, and some other people like very very much to wrap up one thing or another in a certain substance or another . . .

Which is better? Who can say . . .

In fact I can say very definitely which is better, but then if everyone was made the same way the price of clingfilm would skyrocket and everyone would be jostling for position next to Roy and much impoliteness and economic disruption would ensue, so perhaps some cosmic balance is involved.

Also. Briefly I consider putting one of Roy's records on but decide that this may give too big a hint to the contents of the parcel. Instead I put on the fine old party tune "Pop Goes the Weasel."

The game commences and the parcel containing the horizontal Roy is passed around the circle. There is some comment as to the heaviness and speculation that the prize must be large.

"Either that or there are many, many layers to unwrap," says Yul Brynner excitedly. Courteously Jetta is included in the game but

Mitzi passes and unwraps on her behalf as terrapin paws are not adapted to this purpose. Thus in effect Mitzi gets two chances to unwrap in every turn. I can tell this displeases Yul but he is too big a man to forbid it.

I stop the music for the first turn and it is Yul to unwrap. This pleases him greatly.

"Yes!" he cries. "It is me to unwrap! Eat your liver, Morrison," for Jim Morrison has only just passed him the parcel after holding onto it for as long as possible.

In truth I arrange things so that Yul gets to unwrap almost every other turn, for he looks forward to it keenly and when the parcel misses him he scowls and I fear that if he is disappointed he will throw a tantrum and the success of the party will be jeopardized.

However, it is Mitzi, unwrapping on behalf of Jetta, who makes the first significant discovery.

"Also," she says as she removes the next piece of clingfilm and tosses it carelessly aside, "a pair of shoes have been revealed." As Roy's shoes were the last to be wrapped it is unavoidable that they should be revealed first.

"Aha," says Yul. "Perhaps the prize is some large ornamental shoe-tree. I confess I have need of one. It is somewhat irregular that a portion of the prize should be revealed before the final layer has been removed but I cannot deny this will serve to whet my appetite and fire my curiosity."

I return the needle to "Pop Goes the Weasel" and the game resumes with an increased fervor.

As I have used many layers the parcel has the delightful silvery opacity clingfilm will assume after a really thorough wrapping. Nonetheless as the game progresses dark shadows begin to be apparent within the parcel. Then portions of Roy's apparel can be made out, although not his trademark dark glasses, as I took care to obscure them beneath several layers.

"The prize is some clothes," says Mitzi when there are only a few layers left. "It is a suit of dark clothing arranged on a mannequin."

"Nonsense," says Yul. "It is a baroque man-sized shoe-tree, I tell you."

"I can see the face of God," says Jim Morrison in his mystical way. Not to speak blasphemously, but in this case he is not far wrong.

"This is an enigma wrapped inside a mystery," says Yul as they continue to pass Roy around the circle. "I am stimulated to the point of frenzy."

At last, there is but one layer yet to be removed, wound loosely but artfully about Roy. I stop the music just as the Roy parcel lands on Yul Brynner's lap.

"Joy unbounded," he cries. "I shall be the one to rend the final veil. Commiserations, Mitzi. Writhe in my dust, Morrison."

But just as he reaches out to remove the wrapping, Roy does not so much burst forth as sit up.

"Surprise," he says.

The reaction is gratifying.

Yul Brynner gasps in astonishment and then breathes some obscure exclamation originating from the wild Slavic steppes of his youth.

Mitzi shrieks in startlement and then claps her hands and gives vent to peals of merry laughter.

"Whoa, headfuck," says Jim Morrison.

Yul stares silently at Roy for some moments, his mouth hanging open. Finally he throws back his trademark bald head and laughs mightily.

"Congratulations, Roy," he says at last. "It is an unparalleled jape the recollection of which will warm my innards so long as breath moves my body."

"Thank you," says Roy. "May I now get off your lap?"

"You may do so." Roy does so and takes up his seat on the couch again. Yul claps his hands. "Flunkey! Take a message to the editors of the *Düsseldorf Zeitung* at once. I wish to take out an ad in the announcements column. The text is to run as follows: 'I, Mr. Yul Brynner, the well-known bald actor, am not speaking boastfully, but I wish it to be known that on this night at my pied-à-terre in Düsseldorf there occurred the greatest party of all time. Present were Mr. Jim Morrison, Miss Mitzi Klavierstuhl, Jetta the terrapin, Ulrich Haarbürste, several flunkeys, and special guest of honor Mr. Roy Orbison, the undisputed Mr. Fun of the entertainment kingdom. If any man dares question this assertion I will not hesitate to fight him after the traditions of the wild Slavic steppes of my youth.'"

The flunkey scurries off and Roy bows his acknowledgment.

Jim Morrison is still plainly awestruck by the prank.

"He was a parcel," he says, "and then he was a man. This must be some uncanny kind of magic." He picks up a piece of clingfilm and examines it with rapture. "What is this groovy substance of glittery translucence?"

"It is called clingfilm," I say.

"Clingfilm," says Jim Morrison, "wild." He examines the clingfilm wide-eyed with a fascination I know all too well. I cannot blame him and yet I almost think to warn him not to start on that path, to tell him what a demanding mistress Lady Clingfilm can be . . .

Suddenly he leaps to his feet. "Do it, man," he cries. "Do it to me!"

"I beg your pardon?" I say.

"I want to take that trip too!" says Jim Morrison excitedly. "I want you to wrap *me* in clingfilm!"

My palms sweat. I wish to die. The thought of wrapping Jim Morrison in clingfilm is too horrible to contemplate . . .

Now here is a cliff-hanger to kill for! What can happen now? Will I be forced to wrap Jim Morrison in clingfilm or will something occur to forestall this foolish and hideous travesty? Do not expect mercy from this quarter, for I am resolved not to tell you until the next chapter. I confess the power has gone to my head and I am tempted to forbid you to read it for two weeks at least. But I will not do so.

Chapter 14

I resume without ado as it would be the rankest impoliteness to tarry with preamble after such a shocking cliff-hanger.

"Do not be so foolish," Yul Brynner snaps at Jim Morrison. "You are like the emulous dog in the fine old Düsseldorf fable who wished to be an octopus and was covered in humiliation. One clingfilm wrapping is more than enough for any party." Here I disagree with Yul but as he is the host it would be impolite to say so. "This is like the debacle that occurred when you attempted to outshine Johannes Doppelzimmer in the use of joy buzzers and merely shook a lot of hands to no great effect. You will instead give us a party piece of your own devising."

Jim Morrison hangs his head in acknowledgment of the rebuke. "I will do so," he agrees.

"Yes, come," says Mitzi, "had you not promised to regale us with a shamanistic dance?"

"That is so," says Jim Morrison, brightening. "It is guaranteed to make any party go with a swing. It will also send you on a spiritual journey and put you in touch with cosmic powers and previous lives."

There are murmurs of polite interest from all but the nibbling Jetta.

"But hold," says Jim Morrison. "In order to perform a shamanistic ritual properly I require a snake."

"*Ach*," says Yul, "regrettably I am without one. Perhaps my dachshund draft excluder might suffice?"

"At a pinch it would," says Jim, "but on second thoughts I will simply wave around some streamers of this groovy clingfilm substance, if there are no objections to that."

"We do not object," says Yul. "Commence."

Jim nods and commences to wave two ribbons of clingfilm about his head and undulate and gyrate and give vent to strange tribal ululations.

"Feel the vibe," he says. "Embrace the groove. Pay diligent attention to the mystical essences."

He starts to hum and chant as he sways. The shards of clingfilm glitter, captivating, mesmerizing, crystallized strands of ether, neither solid nor liquid but something in between . . .

"Reach out to your inner self," says Jim Morrison hypnotically. "Pierce the veil that hides hidden things. Rap smartly upon the knocker of your door of perception . . ."

I feel my eyes grow heavy. Next to me I see Jetta stop eating and seem to nod her head in time to Jim's rhythms . . .

"There is a footstep in the hall . . . the door is opening . . ."

Mitzi is rapt. Roy's eyes are unreadable behind his dark glasses. Yul Brynner has his eyes closed and his arms folded with concentration.

"Pass beyond the threshold. Wipe your shoes upon the mat. Take off your overcoat and mittens if you are wearing any. You are walking down a long hallway . . ."

My eyes have closed. All there is is Jim's murmuring voice and the gentle swish of the clingfilm streamers as he waves his arms.

"At the end of the hallway is another door. A shimmering white light flickers around the edges. Turn the handle and pass beyond . . ."

And it is so—I seem to see such a door. I knock politely and enter the light . . .

"The secrets of the past and the future are laid out before you. Embrace what visions may come."

And to my bemusement, I do indeed have a most unusual vision, which I will describe for you now . . .

Chapter 15

It starts in Ancient Egypt. I am standing outside my pyramid sweeping sand off the doorstep when he walks through the gate, that well-known Pharaoh of the Upper and Lower Nile, Ra-Ibis-Son.

"Hello, Ra," I say. "What are you doing visiting your tomb?"

"Ensuring all is prepared for my eventual demise," he says.

"Ah," I say. "Would you like to come in and view the death chamber?"

"Indeed," says Ra.

Although he is the pharaoh of all Ancient Egypt and I the high priest of his sepulchre I decide to venture a little joke. "It is somewhat irregular as you have made no appointment and you are very far from dead!"

The Great Pharaoh of Upper and Lower Egypt does not laugh. His eyes are unreadable behind the black obsidian eye guards he wears to ward off the harsh desert sun.

He says, "Apart from a slight sniffle I am in the best of health but no man can plan for the random malice of our various beast-headed gods."

"It is so," I agree.

Ra-Ibis-Son follows me inside his sepulchre, bending as he enters the low doorway so as not to dislodge his trademark pharaonic headgear.

I lead him through several tunnels, conversationally pointing out the various traps and barriers that will protect him from tomb robbers and the ample storage facilities.

We also make urbane small talk about the level of the Nile and the prospects for the bulrush harvest and so forth.

In the death chamber my giant scarab beetle Khetta comes scuttling out to greet us. Neatly stacked piles of gold treasure gleam in the lamplight and there are sundry murals depicting the pharaoh enjoying scenes of sport and frolic in the afterlife. A large sarcophagus waits invitingly and implements for pulling Ra's brain out through his nose and various other organ removals are kept ready in a gaily painted plant pot.

"This is a well-kept pyramid," says Ra-Ibis-Son. "Even your scarab beetle is highly polished."

I bow my acknowledgment. "As your high priest it is my duty to keep everything spick and span."

"It will be a pleasure to be entombed here."

"And let us not forget, completely covered in various preserving substances," I say. "Although not for many years, let us hope," I feel obliged to add.

"Yes," says Ra, "I will be spending all eternity here but I am in no rush to begin."

Just then there is an earthquake and huge blocks of stone come tumbling down around the entrance, sealing us inside the pyramid.

"Also," I say, "it appears we are trapped."

"*Ach*," says Ra, "one of our pantheon of beast-headed gods has screwed me."

"This is highly irregular," I say. "You are entombed here forever and yet you are not dead!"

"There is no sense fighting the will of the beast-headed gods," says Ra-Ibis-Son philosophically. "You must proceed with the preservation rituals as best you can."

"Very well." I bow and fetch my instruments. "First I am supposed to pull your brains out through your nose with a hook."

"We will dispense with that part but you may trim my nasal hair if need be."

"Very well." Suddenly I gasp. "But hold! I regret to report there are no bandages with which to mummify you! Ordinarily I am careful to lay in a good supply but just lately a troop of Ancient Egyptian proto–Girl Guides came by and borrowed them all to practice their first aid with," I lie plausibly.

"So?" says the Pharaoh Ra. "This is surely an annoyance. Without bandages how are you to apply the sundry preserving substances to me?"

"There is no way," I say. "Now your various limbs will rot off and you will be unable to take part in the sports and frolics of the afterlife."

"*Ach*," says Ra, "vexation upon vexation."

I tickle Khetta's clicking mandibles thoughtfully and clear my throat. "There is one thing we might try," I say.

"Name that thing."

"As you know I am something of an alchemist in my spare time," I say. "Not to speak boastfully but I have lately discovered a substance that may be accounted the eighth wonder of the ancient world. Imagine if you will a sheet of silver beaten to an incredible thinness, more a thing of gossamer than a foil. You will scarcely credit it, but this miracle of ancient alchemy is both a bandage AND a preserving substance all in one. Moreover it is transparent, so not only will it preserve you forever but generations unborn would be able to gaze upon your features."

"Unglaublich," says Ra-Ibis-Son. "In such a shroud I would be the envy of the underworld. Does this gift of the beast-headed gods have a name?"

"In simple hieroglyphics, it may be rendered 'The filmy all-in-one bandage AND preserving substance that clings to what it touches with an almost criminal sensuality.' I call it film-cling for short."

"Also," says Ra-Ibis-Son. "Then the way is plain. You will embalm me in 'film-cling' immediately."

"At once, mein Pharaoh."

I fetch the scrolls of film-cling from their sacred caskets and set to work. I wrap him snugly with a millimetrical precision and a workmanship designed to last for the ages. Soon, Ra-Ibis-Son, Pharaoh of all the Egyptians, is completely embalmed in film-cling. In simple hieroglyphics my joy could only be rendered by a picture of a smiling man levitating and embracing the many-armed disc of the sun.

"You are completely embalmed in film-cling," I report with breathless awe.

"Capital," says Ra, somewhat muffled. "Now to lie here undisturbed for quite some time."

"To keep you company I will remain here and watch over you for the next few thousand years," I say.

"That is kind of you."

Gingerly I lower Ra-Ibis-Son into his sarcophagus although I do not close the lid. With the faithful Khetta by my side I prepare to stand vigil over his magnificently glittering form for many, many years.

"My spirit will not soon forget your helpfulness," says the pharaoh. "I will remember this day through many lifetimes."

"So will I," I say, and my voice seems to echo strangely and the lamplight flickers . . .

And so the strange vision concludes.

But staring at the Pharaoh Ra-Ibis-Son, a sudden thought comes to me: Doesn't he bear a resemblance to someone . . . someone I know . . . ?

But . . . who?

I am not to find out, for the mists of the netherworld close around me . . .

Chapter 16

I awake from the reverie to find myself back in Yul Brynner's living room.

None of it happened after all. Or . . . did it?

The others are also awakened from their trance.

"That was most remarkable," Yul Brynner says to Jim Morrison. "I scoffed beforehand but now I confess you are gifted with some uncanny kind of magic. I saw a vision of the wild Slavic steppes of my youth and saw my old babushka for the first time in many years. I should give her a call."

"As for me, I was granted a glimpse of the future," says Mitzi. "Next Tuesday an unsuspected storm front will creep up on Düsseldorf from the east. The timely deployment of this information will enable me to steal a march on my rival Hroswitha Bienenstock, the weathergirl of *Raus Schnell Düsseldorf.*"

"As for me," says Roy thoughtfully, "I saw . . ."

"Yes, Roy?"

"Sand," says Roy puzzledly. "Lots and lots of sand . . ."

"Also . . . ," I say.

I keep quiet as to my own revelation. Jetta for her part looks abstracted for a moment and then returns to the Pomeranian worms.

The party continues on its merry way. We play musical statues and musical bumps and then the fine old Düsseldorf party game of grease-the-piggy-sideways, which involves a jelly bean being passed around a circle of people by means of spoons gripped between the teeth, while a malign force, the piggy, kneels in the middle and attempts to interrupt the process by batting people on the kneecap with a balloon, also clenched between the teeth. If someone should drop the jelly bean they are forced to perform a forfeit and demoted to the rank of piggy and shamed for their lack of zeal.

As time goes on, however, I start to feel uneasy. Roy and Yul and Jim are playing an impromptu game consisting of seeing who can hold the most jelly beans on their tongue without dropping or swallowing them. Despite the discreet ministrations of the flunkeys there is much litter and disarray. Jetta is face down in a bowl of prime Pomeranian worms while Mitzi Klavierstuhl tickles her paws. This is turning into some scene from the *Satyricon.*

This heady entertainment-world lifestyle is all well and good for those who were born to it and I do not wish to be a party pooper. But as the evening wears on I start to become concerned lest Jetta should acquire a taste for such a lifestyle and start to find the humble comforts of our home stale and profitless. She may even wish to leave me and strike out on her own and become the pampered plaything of some well-heeled gadabout of the beau monde. And then what would become of me?

Just then my worst fears appear to be realized.

"Jetta is such a darling," says Mitzi Klavierstuhl. "I have decided to steal her away from you."

"You may not do so!" I shriek. "Give her back to me at once!"

What will happen now? But here I lower the curtain. With such a cliff-hanger in place a more mercenary author would be tempted to end the book at this point and force you to buy a sequel to learn the resolution. I, however, will merely force you to await the next chapter.

Chapter 17

Only those with a debilitating disease of the brain can fail to remember the denouement of the last chapter. At the risk of discriminating against them I will launch straight into the action without recap.

You will remember, then, that Mitzi Klavierstuhl, dangerously charismatic weathergirl of *Guten Abend Düsseldorf*, had threatened to take Jetta from me and that I had forbidden her to do so.

Adrenaline surges through me. I turn ashen and quiver. Never in my life have I come so close to some impolite and regrettable action. When the foundation of one's very home is threatened a primal instinct seizes one to upbraid and remonstrate with the ferocity of some untamed beast of the hinterlands.

"You will not take Jetta from me!" I declare. "I would venture almost anything to prevent you. Do not think that your gender and celebrity status can protect you from complicated legal proceedings. Though you fled to the very ends of the earth my subpoena would pursue you."

"But Ulchen," says Mitzi with a laugh, "I was only joking."

My palms sweat. I have made a horrendous mistake. I wish to join the French Foreign Legion and attempt to redeem myself beneath the savage suns of Africa. I blush and mumble an apology and compliment her half-heartedly on the subtle nuances of the jest.

Fortunately just then a distraction arrives.

There is a knock at the front door and a flunkey is dispatched to find out who it is.

"Sir," he says to Yul upon return, "I have to report that a reporter from *Rolling Stone* magazine seeks admission. He has got wind of your entertainment and begs to remind you that you promised him a peek into your celebrity lifestyle in return for publicity for your new Magnificent Seven film."

"He may enter," says Yul with a magnanimous wave of the hand. "I do not despise the hardworking gentlemen of the press and will accommodate them where I can."

"*Ach*," says Roy to me, "this constitutes an awkwardness. Undoubtedly this is the same fellow we eluded after the show. If he sees me here he will realize I am not still backstage and that his lonely vigil was thwarted by a stratagem. His wounded pride is likely to translate itself into lukewarm reviews of future concerts. We must leave before he enters."

He rises and bows to Yul. "Thank you for a splendid evening but regrettably I find I must leave now," he says.

"You need not fear this man's arrival," says Yul in surprise. "*Rolling Stone* selects their reporters with an almost Darwinian ruthlessness for conviviality and social ease as well as incisive knowledge of entertainment gossip. He will be no impediment to our gaiety."

"Nevertheless for reasons I prefer not to disclose I must ask you to excuse me."

"Very well," says Yul with another magnanimous wave of the hand, "there can be no objection to your leaving prematurely after you have provided us with such fine amusement. Frankly the party has reached its twilight stages in any case and will not continue much longer lest we become flat and jaded. The only cause for regret is that so little of the food has been consumed. Those of us who are left are not likely to finish it and it will be stale in the morning."

Roy turns to me. "Perhaps clingfilm can help in this situation?"

"No," I say.

I do not by any means object to clingfilm being used to wrap food with, but on the other hand I have a sadly finite supply of it about my person and you cannot tell what more interesting uses for it may befall.

We bow and bid our farewells to the others. Mitzi teases me that she will not let me take Jetta but this time I realize it is a joke and retrieve her from her with grace and good humor.

"*Ach,*" says Roy suddenly. "But how are we to leave without offending the *Rolling Stone* reporter? He is undoubtedly in the hall by this time and ambulating briskly toward us. There is no way to reach the front door without being sighted by him."

Diffidently I say, "There is one thing we might try. . ."

And what can that one thing be? Do not seek to ask, for the end of the chapter is upon us!

Chapter 18

It should be confessed immediately that I played a trick on you at the close of the last chapter. Moreover this was not such a nice trick as the one I perpetrated in an earlier installment, for this time the revelation of the truth will lead not to relief but to disappointment and cheated expectations.

I would ask you to consider, however, that as a novelist it is my duty to stay one jump ahead of you and allow you to take nothing for granted even if at times this means I seem to toy with you as a terrapin toys with a half-dead worm. You should reflect that in the long run this can only lead to your heightened enjoyment by means of increased suspense and tension.

In some sense I too am helpless in this matter, for it is the case that I cannot all the time write the things I would wish to write but must take account of the demands of plot and plausibility. Furthermore life itself is not all happiness and often the best-laid plans are thwarted by mischance and random contingency, and any novelist who did not reflect this truth would be a bungler indeed.

After such a long preamble it would not be surprising if you had now forgotten the contents of the previous chapter, so I will recap.

It was required that Roy and I (to say nothing of my terrapin Jetta) should leave Yul's party without alerting the impending rock journalist to our presence. As he was already between us and the front door this presented certain difficulties.

"There is one thing we might try," I had said.

Alas this thing was doomed not to be tried, for just then Yul says, "If you are hell-bent on escaping notice by this man the only course is to leave by the back door."

"It is irregular but unavoidable in this instance," says Roy. "Auf wiedersehen."

"I warn you," says Yul, "it does not give out on a lighted street but on a dark back alley. I flatter myself I am not without influence in this neighborhood, but I cannot answer for any perils you may face leaving that way."

"We must brave them as we can," says Roy.

And we make to the back door and leave.

By this point we are thinking about bedtime but little do we suspect that our odyssey on this night is only beginning.

Roy and I and Jetta progress down the darkened alley behind Yul's back door and then turn into another.

By the time we commence to navigate a third such alley it comes to us that we do not know where we are heading.

"Roy," I say, "I have to confess that I have lost my bearings."

"*Ach*," says Roy, "for my part I admit that I was following you, even though I was walking slightly in front as befits one of my rock star status."

"Logically if we continue to the end of this alley we are sure to arrive somewhere else," I say. "Perhaps it will be somewhere we recognize."

"Let us hope," says Roy. "I for one am not prepared to countenance an ignominious return to Yul's to admit our perplexity."

But after negotiating several more such alleys it comes to us that we are thoroughly lost.

"*Ach*," says Roy, "the night wears on and we are no nearer to home and hearth. What illogical and inefficient scoundrel designed such an ill-lit and unsignposted labyrinth?"

We come to a sort of crossroads of back alleys and are confronted with three different paths to take. But which one would be wisest?

Experimentally I lay Jetta on the ground and wait for her lead, as I have noticed before that she has something of a homing instinct if you wait long enough. But she appears as disoriented as we.

"I do not wish to speak ungallantly but Jetta is of no use," says Roy. "Even if she knew the way it would take all night to follow her. We must rely on our wits to resolve this conundrum."

"I believe we should head in that direction," I say, pointing to a certain alley.

"And I for my part believe we have already traversed that one. I have not spoken of this yet for fear to alarm you but I believe we are going round in circles and will continue to do so until exhaustion lays us waste or our shoes are rendered unfit for further service."

"This is why one should always keep to the main thoroughfares and designated pedestrian areas," I say. "We have no one to blame but ourselves for our rash madcap venture. The situation appears hopeless. And yet. . .I believe I have the glimmerings of an idea . . ."

Of what do I speak? Will this idea save us or will we pay the price for our foolhardy wandering into the unknown, as did Scott of the Antarctic before us?

Posing the questions I lower the veil; the answers await the next chapter.

Chapter 19

From now on I intend to launch straight into each new chapter without reprising what has gone before.

You will remember that Roy and I were lost in a maze of back alleys in a condition of perplexity as to what direction to take.

"My idea is this, Roy," I say. "You will remember that Theseus was able to navigate the labyrinth by means of a trail of thread."

"I am familiar with that snippet of classical mythology but fail to see its current application, not least as we have no thread."

"It is my proposal, Roy, that we leave behind us a trail not of thread but of *clingfilm*, thus leaving a record of the way we have traveled and enabling us to retrace our steps should we come to a dead end. Clingfilm is ideal for this purpose as, although there is little man-made illumination, I have noted before it has the quality of glinting softly in the moonlight, of which we have a sufficient, indeed an almost romantic, amount."

"The plan is sound," says Roy. "Commence to implement it."

"I will do so."

I take a fresh roll of clingfilm and look about me. Conveniently a fence with narrow wooden palings forms one corner of the junction. I place the roll of clingfilm around one of the poles of the fence so it will thereby act as a spool and unravel as we pull it. I make a test by holding the end of the clingfilm and walking off a few paces and it gives satisfactory results, the mother roll turning on the pole and dispensing clingfilm with a delightful rasp.

I say, "Logically you should be the one to hold the end of the clingfilm as you are walking half a pace in front as befits your rock star status. Moreover I am burdened with Jetta, in as far as a terrapin can ever be a burden rather than a solace."

"It is so," says Roy. "I do not object."

"However," I say, "it is the case that should anyone come across us you may look foolish pulling a delightful silvery streamer behind you, in as far as anyone can ever be made to look foolish by clingfilm. Reflect also that a rock journalist is dogging our steps, and should he track us this far his relentless newshound's curiosity would doubtless inspire him to ask precisely why you were pulling a streamer of clingfilm behind you, and you should be forced to confess you were lost in the back alleys. Such an admission would sow dismay in the ranks of your followers were it to be reported."

"Indeed," says Roy. "If I could not be trusted to lead them through a back street, how can they trust me to lead them along the path of moderate excess to the palace of rock and roll wisdom?"

"There is perhaps one solution," I say. "If I were to tie the end of the clingfilm around your midriff, you would thereby be able to pull it after us without holding it in your hand. Should anyone come across us you would be able to pass it off as some delightful baroque cummerbund."

"Yes," says Roy, "that would be far less foolish."

I take the end of the clingfilm and tie it around Roy's waist. I wrap it around several times and tie it tightly. My hand quivers as I force myself to stop there and not do a full wrap but there would be no justification for it in this instance.

"Your waist alone is wrapped with clingfilm," I report in a small disconsolate voice.

"Admirable," says Roy. "Then let us be off."

We make off down an alley, the clingfilm satisfactorily unraveling on its makeshift spool as it is pulled in Roy's wake. As the clingfilm glimmers in the moonlight he is like some bipedal black-clad snail trailing behind him a delightful silvery track.

After several hundred yards and various twists and turns, however, we are confronted with a brick wall and no further means of progress.

"Vexation," says Roy, "this has proved a blind alley. Thank heaven for the trail of clingfilm. Let us retrace our steps."

"But a thought occurs," I say. "How are we to gather up the clingfilm as we make our return journey? For reasons of neatness alone we cannot just leave it strewn about the ground."

"Nor had I intended to," says Roy. "Naturally I had envisaged gathering it up from the paving as we went."

"But we have traveled quite some way and the amount of clingfilm involved is considerable. By the time we returned to our point of origin it would form a large and unwieldy mass inconvenient for you to carry. Furthermore due to its nigh-miraculous clinging properties this would be difficult to disentangle, preventing our using it again when we try another alley."

"I could perhaps wind it about my forearm as I go," suggests Roy.

"You know," I say thoughtfully, "I believe you are on the scent of something there. But a single limb may not be long enough. And if someone should stumble on us, a fine sight you would look with a large mass of clingfilm wound around your arm! Who knows what depravity people would imagine? Why, it would look as though we had been playing at doctors in the privacy of the back alley."

"You have the gift of seeing clearly," says Roy. "Advise me how to cope with this contingency."

"What I propose is simplicity itself," I say. "If you were to rotate your way up the alley and thereby wind the clingfilm around your whole body, you would in effect be transformed into a magnificent human spindle or bobbin of clingfilm and should, by the time we reach our destination, have gathered it all about you in a way that would be easy to unreel. Of course, as a side effect, you would by that point be completely wrapped in clingfilm."

"How obvious the answer once you have explicated it," says Roy. "The way is plain. I will rotate up the alley in such a way as to wrap the clingfilm around me immediately."

Roy starts to make his way up the moonlit alley with a rotating motion. He is like some gyrating houri spinning tempestuously into a diaphanous veil. Such a spectacle the streets of Düsseldorf have never seen. I deftly guide the line of clingfilm as he reels it in about him so that it is distributed evenly about his body. I play it about his torso and his legs and his trademark dark glasses. Soon, Roy Orbison is a human roll of clingfilm. I sigh with fulfillment and reflect that the universe has reached its culmination and the stars may now be packed away.

"You are completely spooled with clingfilm," I announce.

Roy makes muffled noises.

"Now to try the next alleyway," I say, pointing. "If you rotate in the opposite direction you will in effect unspool and leave another trail of clingfilm behind us."

Roy makes noises that sound like "I will do so."

He rotates his way down another alley, shedding clingfilm as he goes. The sight is almost unbearably poignant and yet nonetheless diverting. He is like some anthropoid spinning top that has had the good fortune to be caressed and flung to gyration by some magnificent whip of clingfilm.

All too soon the clingfilm is all unwound from him. However, by this point we find we have reached the end of another alley and again it is a dead end.

"*Ach*," says Roy. "Thwarted once more."

"Yes," I say. "It seems there is nothing for it but for you to repeat your spinning-into-the-clingfilm operation and again retrace the way back to the beginning."

"I will do so," says Roy.

Again Roy commences to rotate back up the alley and transform himself into a magnificent human bobbin of clingfilm. As I guide the clingfilm up and down him we are like the Nureyev and Fonteyn of some splendid clingfilm-based ballet. Soon, Roy Orbison is again completely bobbined with clingfilm. I bow my thanks punctiliously to the everlasting gods and remember to note this day in my diary with two red asterisks.

"You are completely bobbined with clingfilm," I announce, "and we have again returned to our starting point."

Roy makes a noise that sounds like "Also."

"Logically the next alley must grant us exit from this urban warren, for of the four paths to choose we have already tried three if you include the way we came," I say. "If you will unspool again in this direction I am sure our ordeal must be over."

Roy makes noises of assent.

Again he rotates down an alley, divesting himself of clingfilm as he spins. It is like the unfurling of some clingfilm-based party blower of the gods.

Before too long he is again reduced to the sad remnant of past glories tied around his waist.

We have not reached the end of the alley, however, and Roy continues to plod along it for some way, pulling the thread of clingfilm behind him.

But soon a surprising discovery awaits us.

"Oh no," I say, "I have a regrettable report to make, Roy."

"Do not hesitate to make that report," says Roy. "Bad news is best conveyed immediately. Delay can only worsen the sting."

"Then I must report that due to some improbable mischance we are heading back the way we came. I recognize a dustbin we passed not long after leaving Yul's."

"Also," says Roy, "this is an unexpected disappointment. A man of lesser character might issue a profanity in this situation."

"I cannot think how this happened," I say. "In my excitement at the prospect of escape from this situation I must have mistaken the direction."

"The apportioning of blame is futile," says Roy. "Let us console ourselves that once we return to the crossroads only one possible path remains to us."

"Then if you will once again commence your spinning into the clingfilm routine?"

"I will do so."

Once more Roy rotates back the way we came, wrapping himself in the clingfilm. He is like some happy submariner caught up in the tentacle of some resplendent clingfilm sea monster. Soon, Roy Orbison is again completely wrapped in clingfilm. The weight of years lifts from my shoulders and I am born anew, clean, fresh, almost infinitely vulnerable.

"You are completely wrapped in clingfilm," I say, "and incidentally we are once more at the crossroads of the alleys."

Roy makes noises.

"Yes," I say. "If you will unreel that way . . . "

One more time Roy commences to unreel his way down an alley, shedding clingfilm behind him. He is like some black-clad butterfly rashly emerging from some magnificent cocoon of clingfilm into a harsh cruel world.

Before too long he is again thoroughly divested of clingfilm.

"Now to escape from these alleys," says Roy.

It is not to be, however, for right in front of us the alley comes to a dead end!

"Logic and reason have failed us," says Roy in a small quiet disconsolate voice. "The Enlightenment was a lie and we are but the playthings of malevolent forces beyond our ken."

"This is the first alley we attempted to navigate with help of the clingfilm tether," I say. "In our excitement at imminent escape I fear one of us has again made a mistake and chosen the wrong path. There is nothing for it but to again return to the crossroads by means of—"

"Yes, yes, I will again spin into the clingfilm," says Roy.

For a fourth time Roy commences to rotate back the way we have come in such a way as to reel the clingfilm around him. He is like some Chinese ribbon dancer with the good taste to wield a marvelous state-of-the-art transparent ribbon. Soon, Roy Orbison is yet again completely spooled with clingfilm. O Düsseldorf, I think, O mother of prodigies! All ages shall account you blessed for this day's work.

"You are completely wrapped in clingfilm and we have once more arrived at the junction of the ways," I announce. "Now. We know the way we have just come, and I believe the alley opposite is the one we tried before that. Further than that my memory will not stretch. But we are left with two alleys which may grant us egress. I propose we try one and leave Jetta here in front of the other as an aide-mémoire, so that in the event the first we try is a failure there will be no mistaking the one that is left."

Roy makes noises that may be "The plan is sound." I place Jetta in front of one alley with reassurances that we will not long be gone. Roy commences to unspool himself up another.

All too soon he is yet again divested of clingfilm. And yet again we find we have reached a dead end.

"Oh well," I say. "At least now we can positively, absolutely be sure that the final remaining alley must be the one we want."

"I strive to share your optimism," says Roy. "I will once more rotate my way back to the crossroads in such a way as to gather the clingfilm about me."

For a further time Roy Orbison spins his way back to the junction in such a way as to spool the clingfilm about him. From above he must resemble some lucky yo-yo on a clingfilm thread. Soon, Roy Orbison is yet again completely wrapped in clingfilm. Were I to enter a yodeling competition at this moment I would undoubtedly be the winner.

"You are, again, entirely wrapped in clingfilm," I note.

Now we are back at the junction where Jetta waits patiently marking the entrance to another alley.

"Unless some horrendous mischance has occurred it seems certain that this alley is the way we want to go," I say.

Without further ado Roy commences to unreel his way down that alley. All too soon he is again bereft of clingfilm.

However, it then becomes apparent that a horrendous mischance has indeed occurred.

"Oh no," I say, "I have some terrible information. I almost fear to tell you."

"He who shoots the messenger will soon find no one brings him news," says Roy wisely. "Do not hesitate to impart your information."

I say, "I have just now recognized the same dustbin as we saw last time. We are again heading back toward Yul's."

Roy is silent for a time.

"I confess to some chagrin," he says. "How could this mischance have come about?"

"I can only think that while we were in the other alley Jetta must have moved slightly. If this is the case then she has neglected her duty as a marker."

"Let us not blame Jetta," says Roy magnanimously. "It is in a terrapin's nature to move slightly. I acquit her of any malfeasance."

"That is generous of you, Roy."

"Nevertheless this comes as a heavy blow. It is all up with us, old friend. It seems we are fated to roam these alleys like lost souls until the end of time."

"Perhaps we had better settle down here for the night," I say. "We would be at the mercy of the elements but I am sure if I put my mind to it I can think of some way of keeping us warm. Perhaps I can improvise . . . something to wrap around us . . ."

"I for my part am resolved to escape these alleys or die in the attempt," says Roy nobly.

"You will not die!" I exclaim in alarm. "Never! Not ever! It is by no means possible!"

"I do not literally expect to die," says Roy, "although at this point I confess to some dizziness."

I say, "Then we must quickly put an end to this. Let us think." I think. "You know," I say, "now I come to think rigorously, I do not believe we have tried the right-hand alley yet. Moreover, the streetlamp which can just be glimpsed at the far end of it would seem to indicate that it debouches onto a more frequented thoroughfare."

Roy is again silent for some moments.

"I had not noticed such a lamp," he says. "My night vision is not all it should be owing to the chromatic filtering tendencies of my trademark dark glasses."

"Do not upbraid yourself, Roy," I say. "It is a small distant light, easily missed, so insignificant that I have only just thought to mention it. Perhaps I should have done so earlier."

"In a situation of crisis nothing is insignificant," says Roy. "A decision taken with less than total information is likely to be erroneous. In this instance you have not arranged things with your customary efficiency."

I bow my head in acknowledgment of the rebuke.

"Then if you will once more rotate your way back to the cross-roads in such a way as to gather the clingfilm about you . . . ?"

"With joy and zeal," says Roy.

One more time Roy rotates back the way we have come in such a way as to gather the clingfilm about him with my aid. He is like some whirling dervish spinning across desert sands and into the cool embrace of some silvery river. Soon, Roy Orbison is once more completely wrapped in clingfilm. I am drowning in bliss and would not thank you for a lifebelt.

"You are back at the crossroads," I say, "and as it happens, completely wrapped in clingfilm."

Without more ado Roy commences to unspool down the right-hand alley. He is like some careless urchin thoughtlessly discarding a magnificent silvery scarf his doting mother has wrapped about him.

All too soon he has again shed all of the clingfilm bar the tether around his waist. There has been no mistake this time and the alley seems refreshingly unfamiliar and a streetlamp can indeed be seen in the distance.

"Also," says Roy, "I confess to some relief. Now to gain egress from the alleyways."

"Yes," I say. "But hold! What of the clingfilm left strewn between here and the crossroads? It must of course be gathered. Besides, due to an oversight I left Jetta back there. I fear we must go back one last time."

"*Scheisse*," says Roy.

One more final time Roy rotates into the clingfilm back the way he has come so that it is spooled about him. He is like some thick black stick rotated in a cotton candy centrifuge in such a way as to gather cotton candy about it, except not cotton candy but clingfilm. Soon, Roy Orbison is one more time completely spooled with clingfilm. If I had a hat, I would fling it high in the air and not care where it landed.

"You are back at the crossroads," I say, "completely wrapped with clingfilm."

I sigh and mentally take my leave of the scene of so much happiness.

However, a problem occurs and it seems there is now a price to be paid. For I am faced with the necessity of unwrapping Roy from the clingfilm!

In all due conscience I have no excuse not to do so and yet my very hand balks and writhes back upon me as I strive to begin. I steel myself to the task and force myself to grasp the clingfilm with a view to rending it asunder and then mercifully pass out and collapse lifeless to the ground.

When I come to it is to find that Roy has taken matters into his own hand and is spinning industriously about the little square formed by the junction of the alleys in such a way as to unspool. There is not much room to maneuver and he rebounds off walls a couple of times but at length he succeeds. I repress a whimper as he unties the end of the roll from around his waist.

Jetta is staring at me in concern but I reassure her I am well and rise shakily to my feet.

"I am sorry, Roy," I say. "Regrettably I fainted."

"It is understandable after the tension," says Roy. "Now at last we can bid farewell to this place."

I have already said farewell to this little moonlit urban bower of joy.

I pick up Jetta and we set off up the alley, Roy reeling unsteadily as he goes. He seems to have an urge to continue spinning and occasionally turns right round.

This is the end of the chapter.

Chapter 20

You will recall that after wandering about the back alleys for some time we had at last found a means of egress.

The alley continues for some distance but at the end we find ourselves in a street that is somewhat better lit.

At this point I know where we are but the knowledge gives me no joy. For we find we have wandered into the scary part of town.

I wish that I could write with the zest of Charles Dickens in order that I might adequately describe the scenes of degradation we are faced with. Unkempt figures slink through the shadows, their hair ungroomed and their shoelaces undone.

An unshaven man known to have designed a substandard car coughs politely and requests alms from people he has not been introduced to.

Unlicensed street vendors loudly advertise sausages, which may have been cooked in conditions of less than adequate hygiene.

A coffee shop is open for business although it is past ten o'clock, careless of the fact that anyone who imbibes their wares at this point is unlikely to obtain a satisfactory night's sleep. Through the window I glimpse such dubious patrons as a circus clown, a disgraced town councillor and those who eke out a precarious living as trick-cyclists or yo-yo performers. Students dog-ear text-books before my eyes or agitatedly discuss controversial banking theories, so far forgetting themselves as to speak both at once and rudely jab fingers at each other in their mania. From the open doorway comes the sound of shameless boasting and impolite personal remarks.

The air is filled with the squeaking of badly oiled bicycles and the nervous moans of those who do not have adequate pension schemes. The very street sweepers appear slovenly and badly disposed toward their work and neglect to brush the tricky corners next to doorsteps.

"What mean streets are these?" asks Roy rhetorically.

"I am sorry you should have to glimpse Düsseldorf's dark underbelly in this way," I say.

I hug Jetta tighter, although whether to reassure her or myself I do not know.

Reader, it is a novelist's duty to reflect all aspects of society, and it is not right that you should turn your eyes from such unfortunate souls. But it is certainly understandable that you should wish to. I will have mercy on you now and call an end to the chapter in order that you might have a respite.

Chapter 21

The time has now come to leave myself and Roy for a moment. For now I must tell you of something which I, as a novelist, am aware of, but I, in the story, am not.

A short distance away at a corner booth inside that very same immoral cafe we are regarding with such horror sit two degraded figures. They are very much at home among all the defrocked librarians and proponents of specious banking theories and indeed are far worse than either, if truth were known. Although I in the story am not aware of these men as yet, I as the author must tell you that they are thoroughgoing villains and scoundrels of the deepest dye.

Come, let us listen to their conversation and you shall see.

"Good evening," says one.

"Good evening," says the other.

"Are you well?" says the first.

"I am very well, thank you," says the second.

"That is good," says the first. "Or rather, that is bad, for as a thoroughgoing nihilist all my moral values are inverted and I confess it rejoices me to hear of ill health in others. However, as we are bound by a common purpose I suppose it is welcome news to know that your health is adequate to carry out our nefarious plan."

"Apart from a slight sniffle I am in the best of health," says the second.

"Then I hope you die of your sniffle but only after our plan is concluded," says the first, maliciously if pragmatically.

"I know where you are coming from," says the second. "I for my part cordially hope you fall down an inadequately signposted mine-shaft the second our business is transacted."

The first chuckles magnanimously at this sally. "You are my kind of scoundrel!" he says. They both laugh loudly.

Such villains! What can their meeting portend? Read on and you will see. . .

"So," says the first villain, "we should seek to ensure that our nefarious meeting draws no unwanted attention. To avert suspicion perhaps we should order some coffee."

"But it is past ten o'clock," says the second. "We are unlikely to obtain an adequate night's sleep afterwards."

"*Pah!*" says the first villain contemptuously. "I often drink coffee so late as quarter to eleven. It means I stay up until two in the morning and have to go to the bathroom in the night but I do not care!"

"Well," says the second villain, seeking not to lose face, "I have often gone to bed at four in the morning!"

"And I have often not gone to bed at all!" says the first.

"Also," says the second, impressed. "But your brain must pay the price for it?"

"It is so," says the first villain sadly. "I have botched many crimes because of my contempt for the natural sleep cycle."

"Perhaps," suggests the second villain, "we could order a coffee, but only pretend to drink it?"

"That is wise," says the first villain. "But," he adds, "we will pay for it with a trick coin!"

The two of them laugh hysterically.

Such infamy! I would spare you such degraded scenes if I could, but then my carefully wrought plot would make no sense. The novelist's duty is often an onerous one and I can spare myself no more than you.

I will, however, bring the chapter to a close and thereby grant you another brief respite.

Chapter 22

Some distance along from the cafe the scary street joins onto a somewhat busier road.

"With luck we may obtain a bus or tram nearby," I say.

"I wish to be away from this place with all possible celerity," says Roy. "It is extravagant to the point of profligacy but I intend to hail a taxi."

So we stand on the corner and attempt to hail taxis as they pass. However, none stops for quite some time, either because they are already occupied or because the drivers are scared to stop in such a low neighborhood where people may forget to wipe their feet before getting in.

Meanwhile, back in the low coffee house the two villains continue to talk.

They have bought a coffee and paid for it with a trick coin attached to a length of thread which they have yanked back to them out of the hapless waiter's pocket as soon as he has departed.

"Ha ha ha," says the first villain, "a man can live like a king with a coin such as this."

"Of course," points out the second villain, "we are causing considerable economic irregularity by obtaining goods in such a fashion."

"I do not care," says the first villain, and they laugh.

Practiced at deception, they pretend to drink their coffees with many a smack of the lips and sigh of "Ah, that is the real Joe," but really they have not come to drink but to connive. . .

"So," says the first villain, "you are an evil criminal then?"

"Yes," says the second, "and I take it you are as well?"

"Yes," says the first, "but I do not wish the fact widely advertised."

"It is agreed," says the second. "Secrecy is advantageous in our chosen profession, as is ruthlessness. Anyone who stumbles on our rascally plans or impedes our dirty work must be pitilessly put to death or at least locked up in a dark cupboard for many years."

"I am prepared for that eventuality," says the first. "I confess I even welcome it."

"Many people would decry such an attitude and yet I do not find it in my heart to condemn you, for zeal in our chosen profession almost demands it."

"It is so," says the first. "Not to speak boastfully, but I have done many bad things in my time. I am glad you do not condemn me, for we are outcast and despised by normal people."

"Yes, the villain's life can be a solitary one and moreover offers little in the way of long-term security and pension schemes," says the second villain sadly. "Added to that the hours are irregular and we see little of the world beyond dark back alleys and ill-swept dens. Frankly if I had my time over again I would go into some more pleasant line of work."

"As for me," says the first, "I would still become a villain but I think I might also have some more stable career to fall back on."

"How did you start on the sorry path to villainy?"

"I began in the ordinary way, with littering and cutting in line. I logically proceeded to murder and tax evasion and now I estimate I have done all the crimes there are. I am so hardened in crime that I now take a positive delight in flouting the social conventions. I leave my shoelaces untied, I do not comb my hair, and I am cavalier with the use of umlauts."

"I have not yet become so degraded, although I sometimes neglect to brush my teeth," says the second villain. "Naturally I am glad to find you will stop at nothing, and yet I feel I should caution you against leaving your laces untied. It is a transgression that can bring you no material advantage and may actually do you harm, like crossing the road against the traffic lights."

"*Pah*," says the first villain contemptuously, "I often cross against the lights, for the sheer metaphysical evil of it."

"Also," says the second villain, impressed in spite of himself. "Then you are more hardened in crime than I and in accordance with our topsy-turvy morality I am forced to accord you a grudging respect."

"I accept your tribute," says the first villain. "Come, I will 'buy' you another coffee." He takes out his trick coin and winks and the two of them snigger bad-naturedly. . .

The scoundrels! What can transpire from such a meeting of rogues? One thing is for sure, there is dirty work afoot. But I am keeping you in suspense to ensure a diligent perusal of the next installment. . .

Chapter 23

In the cafe the two renegades are still confabulating.

"To each thing its season," says the first villain at length. "Enough braggadocio and one-upmanship for now. Let us proceed to business."

"Agreed," says the second. "Do you have the instructions from our dark spymasters?"

For these are not just ordinary criminals but spies!

"Yes," says the first. He looks around to ensure they are unobserved and then places a briefcase on the table. "You are to take this and deliver it to a third spy belonging to our organization. I am not allowed to tell you his name."

"You know," says the second, "it strikes me that I do not even know your name."

"That is for the best in our slinking and deceitful profession."

"Nevertheless it would make for greater intimacy and team bonding."

The first villain considers. "Then I will tell you my name on condition you also tell me your name."

"I will do so."

"My name is Heinrich."

"Mine is Wilhelm."

"Ha!" sneers the first villain. "I tricked you! My name is not really Heinrich. Now I know your name but you do not know mine. Admit I have bested you and am by far the most efficient spy!"

"By no means," says the second villain, "for I lied too. My name is not really Wilhelm but Otto."

"Ha! And now I know that your real name is Otto."

"But I was lying again. My real name is not Otto either but something so far undisclosed."

"I do not believe you, Otto."

"Stop calling me Otto, for that is not my name."

"Be that as it may, Otto, your instructions are to take this briefcase and deliver it to our contact. This must be done swiftly and efficiently and without witnesses to the transaction."

"How will I locate him?"

"He will be on the corner of this very street five minutes from now."

"And how will I know him?"

"He will be dressed in black clothing and dark glasses, as befits one of our skulking ilk."

"Also," says the second villain. "Then there seems little problem. I am unlikely to encounter two such people dressed like that. . ."

Little does he suspect the irony that lurks in this remark. . .

Why is it so? Some of you may have an inkling and the rest will shortly find out. You should note the information about the third spy wearing dark glasses and black clothing, as it will be vital soon. Mark this page for reference if your memory is poor, but be sure to use a bookmark rather than dog-earing, for others may wish to read this volume after you. This book may be read for thousands of years and you cannot tell what will befall. Whatever future civilizations may arise, it is certain that people will not like to find a book with dog-eared pages.

So. Now by my zeal for orderly method I have spoiled the carefully contrived dramatic climax of this chapter. Before ending I will reprise:

"He will be dressed in black clothing and dark glasses, as befits one of our skulking ilk."

"Also. . ."

Also indeed!

Chapter 24

We now go back to the corner of the street where Roy and Jetta and I are still attempting to obtain a taxi.

You should bear in mind that, although I as the author am aware of the preceding scene with the two scoundrels, I in the story am not.

"*Ach*," says Roy, "we may stand here all night."

I say, "There is one thing we might try . . . "

"I am not in the mood to hear it," says Roy.

I am somewhat surprised by this reaction but think no more of it at the time.

Just then a man approaches us. He carries a briefcase and wears a trench coat with the collar turned up and a black hat pulled down low over his eyes and has what looks like a false beard, although I do not wish to cast aspersions and suppose he may merely be using the wrong brand of conditioner.

Although I in the story do not know this, this is the man who may be called Wilhelm, or Otto, or something as yet undisclosed.

"Good evening," he says.

"Good evening," Roy and I reply. Jetta merely stares rudely at his beard.

"It is a pleasant night," says the man, "although I am informed it rained earlier."

"It did," I say.

The man strokes his false beard thoughtfully and eyes Roy's dark glasses and trademark black clothing.

Then he glances at me and says to Roy, "Will you walk a few paces with me into those dark shadows over there?"

"For what purpose?" asks Roy.

"I wish to be alone with you."

"Very well," says Roy.

"Wait, Roy," I say in alarm. "I do not wish to cast aspersions, but supposing this fellow has some nefarious purpose in mind?" I bow my apologies to the man, who scowls.

"*Hmm*," says Roy, "it is true we have not established his bona fides. I will not walk into the shadows with you. There is nothing that can be accomplished alone in the shadows that cannot be as easily done before friends."

"Very well," says the man. "If that is how you wish to play it."

And he hands Roy his briefcase. "Take very good care of this," he says, and departs back down the street of ill fame.

Roy and I stand and stare after him while Jetta looks curiously at the briefcase.

"This is highly irregular," says Roy.

How irregular we do not yet know . . .

What can transpire now? You must wait patiently until the next chapter to find out.

Chapter 25

You will remember that a strange man had come up to Roy and handed him a briefcase.

"Here is a pretty kettle of fish," says Roy. "Why should a fellow I do not know entrust his briefcase to me?"

I say, "Without wishing to flatter you, Roy, why should he not entrust it to you? You are eminently reliable. I, too, would entrust my belongings to you and feel them as safe and secure as if they were snugly stowed in the secret emergency cache under my own floorboards."

"I will rephrase my question somewhat," says Roy. "Why should a fellow entrust his briefcase to anyone?"

"I admit myself baffled. We can but theorize. Perhaps he is about to embark on sundry actions for which he requires both his hands free. Or perhaps he intends to enter the low coffee shop we passed and does not wish to take the risk of coffee being spilled upon his case by some wildly gesticulating flat-tax advocate. It may be he is about to spend some minutes browsing in some late-opening shop which sells briefcases, and does not wish to take his current briefcase in for fear he may be accused of shoplifting when he leaves. Perhaps, on the other hand, he is about to visit his grandmother, who on his last birthday misguidedly bought him a Hello Kitty duffel bag to keep his private effects in, and he does not wish to hurt her feelings by showing he prefers the briefcase for this purpose. Then again, it may well be that he has some business to transact in that street, but has just seen that an old school friend fallen on hard times has become an unlicensed sausage vendor there, and does not wish to flaunt his own material success before him in the shape of the case. Who can tell?"

"It is a mistake to theorize without enough facts," says Roy. "Nevertheless your suggestions are plausible. I only wish the fellow had asked me before entrusting me with this charge. Let us hope he returns soon, for the night wears on and we are overdue for our beds."

We wait patiently for the fellow to return and claim his case.

Now we must go back to the man who gave Roy the briefcase, who, you may remember, is a spy.

He has not gone very far down the street when he bumps into someone and, regrettably, knocks him over.

"Pardon me," he says, helping the other fellow to his feet. "I did not see you there, for this street is not very well lit and you are wearing black clothing and dark glasses. If you wish to avoid mishaps of this kind you should wear something more visible. I for my part often wear a bright yellow stripe when out at night, although it was not considered advisable on this occasion for reasons I do not wish to disclose."

"Regrettably I am forced to wear black clothing for reasons I also do not wish to disclose," says the other.

"Also?" says the second villain with polite interest. "You know, this is a remarkable coincidence. I have just come from meeting a man who wore black clothing and dark glasses just such as you are wearing!"

"Unglaublich!" says the man in black. "You know, I think perhaps we should write in to *Guten Abend Düsseldorf*'s 'Spooky Occurrences' segment, for you do not yet know the half of the coincidence. For the fact is, I for my part am on my way to meet a man, and have been told that the man I am to meet will be dressed in a trench coat and false beard such as *you* are wearing!"

"You are making a joke with me!" says the second villain. "If this is true it is spooky indeed and we are but the playthings of sinister forces beyond our ken."

"It is certainly true!" says the man in black. "I am to meet him on the corner just there and he is to hand me a briefcase for reasons I am not allowed to discuss."

"A briefcase?" says the second villain. "But this stretches the boundaries of probability. Greta Sonderbar of 'Spooky Occurrences' will faint when she reads our letter. For the fact is, I have just come from the corner where I have delivered a briefcase to the other man in black!"

Those chumps! Little do they suspect what has happened . . .

However, I will now tell you, the reader, in case you have not yet worked it out. The spy has given Roy the secret briefcase in mistake for this man!

"This is something to tell my grandchildren if I am ever blessed in that way, although regrettably at the moment I am single," says the villain in black. "I swear to you that what I have said is true. I am going to the corner right now to meet a man dressed like you who will give me a briefcase. In fact I am already running late and must go now. I would ask you to accompany me so that you may meet this fellow and see all that I have said is true, but for reasons I prefer not to disclose, if you saw him I would then have to kill you."

"I quite understand, for it is the same in my line of work. But what name should I say if I write to Greta Sonderbar? Testimony from two people will be more convincing than one."

"You may refer to me as Lothar X, although that is not my real name," says the other. "Now if you will excuse me I must go to the corner to meet the man who looks just like you and be given a briefcase. If you attempt to follow me a terrible fate awaits you. Good evening."

"Good evening."

But suddenly a terrible suspicion dawns on the villain in the trench coat.

"I do not wish to cast aspersions, but are you perchance a spy?" he asks the other man. "I have a reason for asking."

"Why yes I am, since you ask, although I do not wish the fact widely known."

"Uh-oh," says the second villain. . .

Chapter 26

Roy and I, to say nothing of Jetta, are still waiting patiently for the man to return and claim his briefcase.

As if the fates wish to taunt us, now a succession of taxis appear and idle on the curb. Moreover it is threatening to rain again.

"Vexation," says Roy. "The fellow has no business keeping us here taking care of his briefcase when it is near bedtime. I itch to be home with slippers and cocoa and *Schlaf Gut, Düsseldorf*."

"I, too, yearn for my virtuous couch of repose," I admit. "To say nothing of Jetta. It is not good to keep her out so late, for it disrupts her routine and may lead her to turn feral. Shall I, then, claim a taxi?"

"Not yet," says Roy. "The fellow is sure to return presently. We must discharge our obligation. If only there was some way to pass the time."

"Perhaps I can think of an amusing game to play," I say. "*Hmm.* There is one thing that springs to mind . . ."

Alas that thing is not to be revealed, for just then there comes the sound of footsteps and a man approaches, although from a different direction than the one in which the man who left the briefcase disappeared.

"Vexation of the highest order!" cries Roy. "Do you see who it is? It is that pestilent *Rolling Stone* reporter!"

It is so.

"Am I then to have no peace? He is not so much a man as a sleuth-hound. He will detain me here half the night seeking to know my views on wah-wah pedals and the Central European Bank. We must move with haste if we are to avoid him. Quick, pile into the nearest taxi before he reaches us."

"But what of the briefcase?" I say.

"The man may advertise in the *Düsseldorf Zeitung* when he wishes it returned," says Roy. "I did not offer to look after it and nor did he seek my permission."

Quickly we bundle into a taxi. The *Rolling Stone* reporter calls out "Mr. Orbison! A word with you, please!" but rudely we feign not to hear him and instruct the driver to move off.

Meanwhile the spy in the trench coat has realized what has happened.

To the spy in black and dark glasses he says, "I must tell you now that we will not be able to write to Greta Sonderbar of 'Spooky Occurrences' after all, for there is a logical explanation for the coincidence. There usually is if one looks hard enough, as Greta takes great care to impress upon people so that they will not think we are at the mercy of forces beyond our ken. For the fact is, I *am* the spy in the trench coat and false beard you were scheduled to meet!"

"Also?" says the spy in black. "But this is most irregular, for we were ordered to meet on the corner rather than in the middle of the street."

"Alas, that is not the only irregularity to occur," says the other. "For due to an oversight I have given the secret briefcase to an entirely different man who was standing on the corner at the appointed time and who was himself wearing black clothes and dark glasses."

"So?" says the spy in black. "Then perhaps we will be able to write to Greta Sonderbar after all, for that in itself is a remarkable coincidence."

"Yes, there is that to be said for it. On the other hand, the giving of the briefcase to someone unconnected with our organization has jeopardized the success of our mission, and should the contents fall into the hands of the authorities our liberty, perhaps our very lives, will be at risk."

"Yes, that is a minus. It was very remiss of you to give the secret briefcase to the wrong man and I believe the fact will be reflected in your next job performance evaluation."

"With all due respect," says the spy in the trench coat, "if you had not been late for the secret meeting the mix-up would not have occurred, or at least I would have had a 50 percent chance of picking the right man."

"I concede my share in the error," says the other fairly. "In my defense I kept walking into walls on the way here due to the poor lighting and the chromatic filtering tendencies of my dark glasses."

"The proper procedure is to report this mistake to our immediate superior," says the spy in the trench coat. "I have just left him in the cafe over there." He refers to the other spy who gave him the briefcase.

"He scares me," says the spy in black. "He is sure to yell at us, or at least employ tones of a silken menace."

"He scares me too," admits the spy in the trench coat, "and yet in accordance with our topsy-turvy morality I am forced to feel a grudging respect." He looks around and lowers his voice. "Did you know he crosses the street against the traffic light for the sheer evil thrill of it?"

"I had heard rumors to that effect but would not have credited them without your testimony."

Reluctantly the two of them make their way to the low cafe and to the booth at the back where the other villain is sitting. He is still amusing himself by buying things with the trick coin attached to a piece of thread and now has yet another cup of coffee and several slices of cake in front of him, none of which he has paid for properly.

"Otto!" he calls loudly, just to embarrass the other spy, who glances around furtively and turns up the collar of his trench coat in case anyone has heard. "Did it go well?" he asks in a quieter voice.

"I have to report that it did not . . ."

"*Ach*," says the first spy as they explain, "this is a catalog of errors. It would seem," he adds in tones of silky menace, "that you have outlived your efficiency."

The two other spies gulp nervously, for in their organization to be judged to have outlived your efficiency does not mean such ordinary things as your desk being moved to the back of the room or being pensioned off with a nice clock or being banished to a distant province: it means death, without even a written warning.

"We must move quickly and with relentless zeal," says the head spy. "The briefcase must be recovered and those who have taken it must be chased and killed!"

"Could they not simply be locked in a dark cupboard for a time?" suggests the second spy. "They seemed to be harmless passersby."

"No, they must be chased and killed, and all their belongings confiscated," says the head spy. "I do not think they were harmless. Why do you think another man dressed in black clothing and dark glasses happened to be standing on the corner at that time?"

"Coincidence?" says the spy in the trench coat and false beard.

"Spooky occurrence?" says the spy in black clothing and dark glasses.

"Or enemy action?" says the head spy, who wears a trench coat and dark glasses, and also a sombrero, for he has just returned from fomenting a revolution in Latin America.

The dark glasses, by the way, are not nice dark glasses like Roy's trademark ones but very evil-looking spy dark glasses.

"Whatever is the truth, the error must be corrected at once. Be they a shadowy cabal of enemies or hapless victims of the random malice of fate, they will rue the day they impeded our plans!"

At this dramatic juncture I allow you to pause for breath. I shall meet you in the next chapter when you have the strength to imbibe it.

Chapter 27

The three villains leave the cafe and make to the end of the street. They are in time to see the taxi containing me and Roy zoom off into the distance.

"*Ach*," says the head spy, "thwarted."

"I suppose we had better go home and accept defeat, then," says the second.

"Is this how you display relentless zeal?" asks the chief villain in tones of icy malice. He is being sarcastic. "You must display more tenacity if you wish to be a fully fledged member of the Secret Society of the Black Skull of Dreadful Death."

The second spy bows his head in acknowledgment of the rebuke.

The spies notice the *Rolling Stone* reporter loitering by the curb, looking after the taxi and tutting. They nudge each other and approach him.

"Pardon me," says the chief spy, "I do not wish to pry, but may I ask why you are looking after that taxi, tutting and looking vexed? I have a reason for asking."

"I do not object to answering your question," says the *Rolling Stone* reporter. "You are prying somewhat, but zeal in my chosen profession requires a certain amount of prying, so I do not find it in my heart to condemn you. The fact is, I wished very much to speak to one of the occupants of that taxi but arrived too late to do so."

"What a coincidence!" exclaims the spy. "My cohorts and I also wished to do so."

"So?" says the *Rolling Stone* reporter. "That is indeed a coincidence. Perhaps we should tell Greta Sonderbar."

"I do not think it is quite that big a coincidence," chuckles the head spy. He decides to venture a little joke. "Now, if the taxi had been driven by the monster of Loch Ness, *that* might be of interest to Greta Sonderbar of 'Spooky Occurrences'!"

But the *Rolling Stone* reporter does not laugh. His eyes express no mirth. Coldly he says, "There are few strangers in the world of show business and I have to inform you that Greta Sonderbar is a platonic friend of mine. She has never stooped to sensationalism such as you describe and I do not appreciate your mockery of her show."

The spy blushes and mumbles his apologies. But inwardly he vows that one day he will deliver a time bomb to the *Rolling Stone* reporter for failing to laugh at his joke—or at the least lock him in a dark cupboard for many days. "And there will be earwigs and damp umbrellas in the cupboard," he mutters spitefully.

"I am sorry, I did not catch that?" says the *Rolling Stone* reporter.

"Nothing, I was continuing to mumble apologies," the villain lies with practiced deception. "Without wishing to pry further, may I ask why you wished to speak with the occupant of the taxi?"

"The reason is simple. I am a reporter for *Rolling Stone* magazine, and I wish to interview that occupant, for he is none other than Mr. Roy Orbison, the well-known rock troubadour and man in black!"

"Also!" say the spies, nudging each other.

Hastily the leader says, "I mean, but of course! And this," he lies easily, "is a coincidence that may well be worth mentioning to your close friend Greta Sonderbar, for the fact is my friends and I also wish an interview with this Orbison fellow!"

"Are you then journalists?"

"But assuredly," says the spy in the sombrero. "I am a stringer for the *Düsseldorf Zeitung.*"

"And I am a correspondent for *Mönchengladbach After Hours,*" says the spy in black.

"And I write for *Just Seventeen* magazine," says the spy in the trench coat.

"Also?" says the *Rolling Stone* reporter. "That is a surprise to me, for I had envisaged the staff of *Just Seventeen* magazine as being mainly comprised of young girls."

"No, it is mainly written by men in trench coats and unusual beards," lies the other quickly. "I have to use my imagination when describing kissing boys or having a crush on pop heartthrobs."

"Perhaps," says the chief spy slyly, "we should pool our intelligence. If you tell us what you know of this Orbison fellow we may be able to work out where we can find him."

"I agree to your proposal," says the real reporter unsuspectingly.

"Where does he live?" asks the villain. "Where does he come from? Does he have any friends, relatives, associates or pets whom he would be grieved to see menaced or locked in a dark cupboard with earwigs? I have a reason for asking."

"It is said he comes from North America originally but nowadays he spends much time at a pied-à-terre in an undisclosed location in Düsseldorf," says the *Rolling Stone* reporter. "Occasionally he winters at Baden with his mother, but they are rumored to be temporarily estranged following an incident in which he neglected to obtain her a Christmas present. As for friends, associates and pets, Yul Brynner, Jim Morrison and Mitzi Klavierstuhl of *Guten Abend Düsseldorf* all speak freely of him as the undisputed Mr. Fun of the entertainment kingdom. Furthermore," he consults a notebook which he has just filled at Yul Brynner's house, "he is known to associate with one Ulrich Haarbürste, who is described as being a local man of commendable diligence. Little else is known of this Haarbürste save that he owns a terrapin, Jetta. While this is not Orbison's pet, he is almost certainly fond of her as she is said to be well-groomed and most ladylike in her behavior, except perhaps when it comes to eating prime Pomeranian worms."

"You have compiled your dossier with commendable zeal," says the first villain.

The reporter bows.

"So," mutters the rogue, "if we cannot contrive to meet Mr. Roy Orbison given this information, we do not deserve to be called spies!—I mean, reporters," he adds for the benefit of the *Rolling Stone* man. "It will not be too long before we pay this fellow a call. . ."

If this were a film, reader, I would add dramatic music at this point. . .

Or would I? Steel yourself, for worse is yet to come. How could it possibly be worse? Read on and you will see. . .

Unsuspecting of our imminent peril, Roy and Jetta and I have driven off in the taxi.

As we pull away I cannot help glancing back guiltily toward the *Rolling Stone* reporter, thwarted in his attempt to ask Roy various importunate questions about plectrums and wah-wah pedals, and am in time to see the three villains reach the corner and hop up and down in frustration as they see us drive off. My breath catches as I glimpse the chief villain's headgear and I frown thoughtfully.

"You know," I say, "I could have sworn I just saw a man wearing the sort of sombrero favored by Mexican bandits."

"So?" says Roy.

"I confess to having a fear of Mexican bandits," I admit.

"Who does not?" says Roy. "If they have extended their activities to Düsseldorf none of us will be able to sleep safely in our beds at night."

Presently we arrive at the street in which we live.

"At last," says Roy, "home and hearth, made more sweet than ever by our sundry travails and annoyances. Who would ever leave if not for the joy of coming back?"

Courteously Jetta and I escort Roy to his gate.

However, it turns out that Roy is not to reach home and hearth so soon after all.

"*Ach*," he says suddenly, "I find I have left my door key on my dressing table at the concert venue. I will not soon be able to gain admittance. How ironic, to be locked out of my own home!"

"So?" I say. "Naturally I would offer you my hospitality for the night, but on reflection I seem to remember that the spare room happens to be piled to the ceiling with boxes of . . . various substances . . . And Jetta's bedroom is being redecorated and she is temporarily bunking with me."

"I can of course walk to the phone box on the corner and order a flunkey to fetch my door key," says Roy. "But it is starting to rain and moreover if I do not soon gain admittance I will miss the beginning of *Schlaf Gut, Düsseldorf*. I am keen to see if Herman Umschlag mentions my concert in his topical monologue."

I clear my throat and say, "There is one thing we might try. If I was to hurl you headfirst through your front window you would be able to gain entrance without resort to the door."

"You have a gift for cutting through the Gordian knots of everyday existence," says Roy. "The plan is irregular on many different levels and yet admirably dynamic. The way is plain. You will hurl me headfirst through the front window at once."

"But hold," I say, "it strikes me that if I do so you risk being injured by shards of glass."

"*Ach*," says Roy, "that is a drawback."

"And yet," I say, "I am confident we can overcome it. If there was some way we could first provide a sort of cushion or protective covering for you, that you may be hurled through the window with impunity. . .If there was something, perhaps, we could wrap you in. . ."

"If only," says Roy.

"One thing occurs," I say, reaching to my inner pocket. "I believe I have the glimmerings of an idea."

"If it involves clingfilm, I do not wish to hear that idea," says Roy.

"It strikes me," I say, "that we have close at hand a substance that . . . I am sorry, what did you say?"

"I said," repeats Roy, "that I will not be party to any idea that involves wrapping me in clingfilm."

I pause for quite a long time. My palms sweat. I do not wish to believe my ears.

Presently I say, "As it happens, I believe I was groping toward a suggestion along those lines. But what can your objection be?"

"I have had enough of clingfilm tonight to last me a lifetime," says Roy. "Although I cannot deny it has been of service to me several times this evening, after our ordeal in the back alleys I am positively averse to the substance. Not only will I not be wrapped in it, I never wish to see the stuff or ever hear it mentioned again!"

There is a long and terrible silence.

After that, things happen, but I barely notice them. Roy walks to the corner phone and summons his roadie. A while later the man appears with the key. Roy opens his door and bids me good night. I respond automatically, or at least I hope I do.

I stand there numbly for some time. Rain falls on my face, random, inconsequential, as meaningless as the rest of this joyless universe. After a time I walk home, mechanically, one foot in front of the other, dimly aware that the next day and every day after I will be required to walk to other places there is no point in reaching.

If this were a film, reader, at this point I would insert the "Funeral March."

Chapter 28

Anyone who has ever wanted very much to wrap someone in clingfilm and then found out that they will never again be able to wrap that person in clingfilm will readily be able to understand my feelings at this point.

Life has lost its savor. There is nothing more to hope for. Everything is flat, stale and profitless. My house seems more like a mortuary than a dwelling place and my very clingfilm cupboards have become unexciting and ordinary items of furniture rather than tabernacles of unending bliss.

Of course I have brought this on myself. I am being punished by the ineluctable gods for wrapping Roy too many times in the alley and making him dizzy. I wring my hands, seized with remorse. I am a cad and a brute. But this—this is too cruel a sentence.

"Is it my fault?" I whisper brokenly, falling on my knees and gazing toward the pitiless heavens, or my neatly painted living room ceiling which is in the way. "Is it my fault he is so damn wrappable? Why did you make him like that," I apostrophize the eternal gods, "if not for me to adorn him in clingfilm?"

I collapse on the couch, a broken and pitiful man. I cradle Jetta for support and she seeks to console me as best she can, looking phlegmatic and stoical as if to suggest that after all not much has changed and life must go on. After a while she gets tired and goes to sleep.

My eyes lose focus and I indulge in reverie. I remember how it was in the old days, the dark days before Roy walked into my life. . .

In those times life was not so pleasant because I did not have the chance of wrapping Roy and all I had were my dreams. And sometimes I told people my dreams and they would become alarmed.

I was lonely at times. People suggested that I take a wife and this seemed to be a thing to do. I made experiments in that line but it did not work out because the woman was not interested in playing certain little games I was interested in playing, dressing-up games and so forth.

One day when I had confessed my dreams to someone it was suggested I should visit a group for those with uncommon desires. At this club people who wish to do statistically unusual things meet to chat about it and reassure each other they are not so strange. To speak frankly, and without wishing to cast aspersions, I find them a bunch of weirdos and hug Jetta to me for protection.

There is a retired police inspector who thinks that the sum of human happiness would be to tickle his own ears with sprigs of parsley while a Latvian cleaning woman with an enormous bosom belches in his face. Although he is filled with shame and fear for his reputation at this unnatural longing, he has hired several such women to clean his house and plies them with gaseous foodstuffs and fizzy drinks but so far has had no joy. The hard bit is to find excuses to lurk around them and always be casually scratching his ears with parsley without arousing their suspicions.

"Last week Lizina did a small burp," he says once, "but she stifled it almost immediately and she was not facing in my direction. Still in my excitement I got parsley lodged in my eardrums."

We commiserate politely on his near-miss.

There is a woman who once had a dream that a bishop with a long nose sidled up to her in a crowded tramcar and slyly put jelly down her dress while humming the *William Tell Overture*. She found this the most erotic sensation ever and now forlornly hopes that it may one day come true and spends many hours optimistically riding trams around Köln Cathedral, to no avail.

There is a man who gets his jollies by walking around town with bananas concealed down his socks and another who likes to bounce around naked on a space hopper. There is a woman who yearns to be erotically but impersonally measured by a building surveyor and there are people of both sexes who enjoy rubbing up against thrumming refrigerators. There are two people who like to pretend they are railway trains while mating—sadly they run on different gauges—and some people who like to do things with cheese.

On the third week it is my turn to confess my desire. When I do so there is a dead silence and several people leave.

I decide to enroll in a nice animal grooming class instead.

One day I become lonely and I place an ad in the personals section of the *Düsseldorf Zeitung*:

"Anyone who would like to be wrapped in clingfilm and is first prepared to have major surgery in order to look like a certain person contact me.

"I intend to keep you wrapped in clingfilm in my front room for a very long time indeed. I promise to make urbane small talk so as not to make the ordeal unpleasant for you and to dust you when needed.

"Must be fond of terrapins."

There are no respondents.

At one point, for reasons I prefer not to disclose, various complicated legal proceedings arose and it was recommended that I visit a doctor of the brain.

He was a pleasant and courteous man and I did not mind our talks but often they were baffling to me. But they appear to have been more baffling to him, for he could not understand why I liked certain things so much and why I had the urge to do certain things. He said he wanted to write a book about me and often he would invite his colleagues in to look at me. But in the end he became unhappy and retired from being a doctor of the brain.

I remember we played a pleasant game where he would show me cards with blots of ink and I would have to say what I thought they looked like.

"What does this blot remind you of?"

"Roy Orbison."

"And this?"

"Roy Orbison, in clingfilm."

"And this?"

"That is a scary and menacing blot. It is a bad man who wishes to confiscate my clingfilm."

"And that?"

"That is obviously a hippo emerging from a mud wallow."

"Aha! Now we may be getting somewhere. Tell me about the hippo. What does the hippo want?"

"Who can tell what a hippo wants?"

"Visualize the hippo. Where does the hippo go after leaving the mud wallow?"

"It trots a short distance into the veldt where Roy Orbison and I are on safari. It prepares to shake itself briskly to get rid of the mud. Roy will obviously be covered in mud unless it is somehow prevented. I propose to cover him in clingfilm and he assents."

"I see." The doctor sighs and looks disappointed. "What is this blot?"

"That is a scary and menacing blot. It is a Mexican bandit who has come to steal my terrapin."

And so on. The doctor would often appear unhappy and confused and sigh a lot after these games. If his colleagues were there they would stare at me for a very long time.

Once he asked,

"May I ask why you brought your terrapin to this appointment?"

"It would hardly be humane to leave her in the car."

The doctor drummed his fingers on the table.

"But why did you put her in the car in the first place?"

"Because I was getting into the car to come here."

"Yes but . . . do you take Jetta everywhere with you?"

"Not everywhere. I do not usually go far outside Düsseldorf."

"Everywhere you go?"

"But naturally."

This made him sigh too.

Once the brain doctor developed a theory and became excited. He said:

"Perhaps this American rock star represents the wild and uncontrollable life force. In seeking to confine and sanitize him, you are actually seeking to repress your own dark urges."

By now I had had enough. I rose and made a little speech which embarrassed me at the time but which afterwards I was glad to have made. I said:

"I do not wish to cast aspersions, Doctor, but you have the soul of a textbook and are without poetry. No man can plumb the mysteries of the human heart and some things cannot be explained by your blots and your test tubes and your obsession with the unmentionable parts. I do not know why I wish to wrap Roy Orbison in clingfilm, but I know that it is what I was born for and that it would be a very beautiful thing to do."

And I bowed coldly and left.

Jetta was the only one who understood, and I am not sure even she understood completely. Still, a terrapin will not judge you as long as you feed her worms and take her for walks occasionally and redecorate her bedroom when she seems dissatisfied with it.

But even in those dark days there was always the hope that one day I would meet Roy and that he would allow me to wrap him in clingfilm.

Now that hope has been and gone. There is nothing left for me. In the extremity of my despair I contemplate committing suicide.

Of course the problem would be the disposal of the body. It would be impolite and unhygienic to leave it for someone else to find.

I consider drowning myself in the ocean but then remember I cannot swim. I would therefore be unable to get far enough out to ensure my body would not be washed up on shore or tangled up in someone's paddleboat or give a sudden unwelcome shock to someone floating happily on a pool mattress. I consider jumping off a cruise liner far out at sea but my absence at the dinner table would be remarked upon and I would put the stewards to much trouble searching for me. I could of course leave a note but the captain, chefs and so forth would doubtless believe my death was due to some failure on their part and so become a prey to gloom and despond.

Another plan that occurs is to kill myself after first tying myself up inside a trash bag. This would be left on the doorstep in the ordinary way for disposal by the designated authorities. At first this seems an excellent solution. I fetch trash bags and after several attempts learn how to tie them up from the inside while I am curled up within them. There is then some difficulty in releasing myself from the bag. When I do so I see Jetta has woken up and is watching me. She does not look approving. In fact she gives me a look such as the brain doctors would give me or such as my wife would sometimes give me before our divorce.

I realize I will have to tie myself up inside the trash bag outside on the street, as once I am inside the trash bag I will not be able to open the door and leave. However, it cannot be tonight, as it is not the designated night to leave the refuse outside. I may have finished with life myself, but that is no reason to disfigure the streets for others. Moreover there remains the problem of how to kill myself once I am inside the trash bag. I could secrete a knife and stab myself in the organs once I am neatly tied up. But I reflect that it would not do to dispose of a sharp object like that in a trash bag as the trash collector might cut himself upon it. The problem seems insoluble.

Then I reflect on Jetta. Am I to leave her alone in the world? Mitzi Klavierstuhl would doubtless agree to look after her, but I am afraid her fast ways would corrupt Jetta. The only one I could trust to nurture her properly would be Roy. And without wishing to cast aspersions, even he would often be too busy with his rock star duties to have time to attend to her needs. He would doubtless have to delegate her to some uncouth roadie and she would end up some neglected backstage pet, toted round carelessly from arena to arena with the plectrums and the wah-wah pedals.

And what of Roy? Would he not be wracked with guilt upon my demise? It would not be fair to him. The more I reflect the more I realize that I have been upon the verge of an impolite and regrettable action. I decide to go to bed.

Somehow I manage to sleep a little but the next morning brings no relief from my misery. It appears I must go on living but my heart is not in it. I rise five minutes late, neglect to make my bed, and only brush my teeth casually. I even leave my shoelaces untied out of contempt for the universe. By this point in my decline I am no better than some unpleasant and dangerous beast.

However, I trip over my laces and bang my head and realize I am only harming myself by these transgressions. I must pull myself together. I must find some new purpose in life even if it is an arbitrary one.

Then suddenly I see it, the answer to all my problems: I will join the French Foreign Legion!

Immediately this resolution bucks me up somewhat. It is the perfect answer.

I am leafing through the phone book for the number of the recruiting office and musing to myself on how Jetta will look in a French Foreign Legion hat when there is a knock upon the door.

To be continued . . .

Chapter 29

I open the door. Roy stands there upon my threshold in his trademark black garb and dark glasses. It feels as though it has been a thousand years since we parted, but in fact it has not been. He is the same as ever, and yet all is terribly changed.

"Hello, Roy," I say trepidantly. "What brings you to my house?"

"I am seeking to borrow a cup of sugar," says Roy.

"So?" I say. "I am happy to oblige."

I fetch the sugar from where I keep it in the back garden shed, the kitchen cupboards being filled with a more important necessity.

"Alas, my cups are in the dishwasher, and it would be irresponsible to interrupt it in the middle of the cycle," I say. "Perhaps I could improvise a small parcel or twist of sugar by wrapping some in clingfilm." I pause and eye him keenly. "If you do not violently object to that," I say wryly.

Roy makes a distracted gesture. "The need is not pressing. I am content to wait for the dishwasher to fulfill its natural course. Indeed I confess the request for sugar was a ruse. I had hoped for the opportunity to linger and indulge in polite chit-chat."

"Very well," I say, somewhat frigidly. "Although I am not sure what there is to say to each other."

"I had envisaged making urbane small talk on topical matters of the day."

"Also? I will endeavor to oblige. Of course I am a rather stupid person who has ideas about wrapping people in things they do not wish to be wrapped in, so my talk may not be very urbane," I say somewhat bitterly.

"I will make allowances," says Roy abstractedly.

I raise an eyebrow and nod.

"Then if you will please to sit."

"I will do so."

Roy Orbison sits down on my couch. I sit opposite and drum my fingers on Jetta agitatedly.

"Hroswitha Bienenstock on *Raus Schnell Düsseldorf* predicted a fine day," says Roy as an opening gambit. "She is not so reliable as Mitzi but is generally to be depended upon."

"I hope she is squashed by a falling meteorite," I say.

"Also?" says Roy, his trademark glasses not quite masking his surprise. Jetta, meanwhile, seems to stiffen with shock beneath my touch, although it is hard to tell because of her terrapin carapace. "That is an unusual desire. Perhaps an inaccurate prediction of hers led to a ruined picnic or dampened shopping expedition once?"

"I have no personal animus against her but she is a pointless person, not even aware of her own pointlessness, just like everyone else in this wretched municipality," I explain. "The whole of Düsseldorf should be smothered in volcanic lava or devoured by a giant sea monster that has wandered too far inland."

"Also?" says Roy. "That is an unorthodox point of view."

"It is, but I cling to it tenaciously. Furthermore if you say 'Also?' once more I will rip my own ears off and stuff them up your nostrils."

There is silence for a time. Roy sits impassively like an unfeeling, uncaring, insensitive brute of a black-clad stone statue.

"I believe the dishwasher has finished," he says at last.

"I hope it is trampled and violated by Mongol horsemen," I say spitefully.

The room seems to spin around me. I am appalled at my lapse from urbanity but I do not seem able to help myself. I appear to have turned into some unreasoning beast of the hinterlands. With an effort I pull myself together.

"Forgive me, Roy, I am not myself today. The fact is I have recently suffered a disappointment that has killed all my joy in life, but I should not have taken it out on you. I am at a loss how to atone for this lapse unless I join the French Foreign Legion and work out my penance fighting hand-to-hand against endless waves of unkempt dervishes."

"And I may come with you," says Roy quietly.

"You?"

"The fact is the request for polite chit-chat was also a ruse. I sought out human company since my own was unbearable. I am consumed with remorse for my lapse from manners last night."

"Also. . ." I say. I affect nonchalance and stroke Jetta's nose idly. "That is most interesting. Pray continue."

"Yes," says Roy, rising and pacing. "In effect I deprived that man of his briefcase through my heedless impatience to be off. Moreover I was unconscionably rude to the *Rolling Stone* reporter. If I disdain the hardworking gentlemen of the press I will lose touch with my fan base. I seem doomed to become an incurable egotist, recording sprawling three-hour experimental albums and trampling infants in the street." He stifles a moan and wrings his hands.

This was not the confession I had expected or hoped for, but I am moved by my friend's agony and instantly set aside my own.

"Roy," I say, "you are the most punctilious person I know. Any errors were due to tiredness and the random abrasions of a busy day. It will be easy to make amends."

"Then you will help me?"

"But of course, Roy, that is what friends are for." I am ashamed of my own selfishness. I am a small and reprehensible man. Roy is not just some almost criminally fascinating entity it is good to wrap in clingfilm. He is a person in his own right with hopes, fears and neuroses of his own. It comes to me that, all this time, I, ironically, have been the one that has been completely wrapped—in obsession . . . !

I stifle a moan of guilt. Perhaps only now am I coming to maturity.

"I will help you in any way I can."

"Capital," says Roy. "Let us be off then. The first step is to return the man's briefcase."

I rise and bow. "I will be ready in one moment."

I head to the kitchen and take several fresh rolls of clingfilm from the refrigerator. After all, you never know . . .

Chapter 30

You may remember that Roy had implored my help in putting right his various social transgressions.

I may not, alas, dwell on this happy scene of reunion between Roy and myself, for the demands of my carefully crafted plot mean I must now return you to the three sordid villains.

You are, of course, cognizant that, while I as the narrator am perforce aware of their shenanigans, I in the story am not.

The three evil spies have arranged to meet the *Rolling Stone* reporter for breakfast at one of Düsseldorf's many delightful open-air cafes.

These cafes and sunlit boulevards, I should reassure readers, are far more characteristic of Düsseldorf than the naked brutality of the scary part of town, which I confess owes something to my imagination. At any rate I have never been there. While my story demands a seasoning of seediness, I would not wish to basely slander my home or fall afoul of the gentlemen from the Düsseldorf Chamber of Commerce. You may visit Düsseldorf in or out of season and, provided you stick to the main thoroughfares and designated tourist attractions, you are unlikely to be molested by spies or threatened with an unlicensed sausage or encounter such harrowing scenes of degradation as I have described. If you wander off the beaten track, though, I cannot answer for what may befall—although that is true for anywhere.

"Good morning," says the *Rolling Stone* reporter to the conniving villains he believes to be fellow journalists. "Did you sleep well?"

"I did, thank you," says the spy in the trench coat and false beard, although this morning he is no longer wearing a trench coat but an ordinary tweed suit and has changed his false beard for reasons of hygiene. "I obtained a full eight hours and am fresh as a petal."

"I slept well too, although I only managed seven hours," says the spy who wore dark glasses and black clothing. This morning he is still wearing dark clothing, although a different suit of it, but has changed his dark glasses for a sinister monocle.

The first villain chuckles pityingly and says, "I sneer on the need for sleep. I closed my eyes for a few minutes around dawn but I never really lost consciousness."

He is still wearing his rather soiled and crumpled trench coat and Mexican hat, as he has not even been to bed.

"Also," says the *Rolling Stone* reporter, surprised. "But such behavior must take its physical and mental toll?"

"It is so," admits the villain sadly. "I have missed out on many brutal political assassinations—I mean, exclusive newspaper scoops— due to my devil-may-care attitude toward circadian rhythms. I once fell asleep in the afternoon and so missed the climax of the council's debate on the rezoning bill," he adds casually, for he is a practiced liar.

Once the habit of lying takes hold of you it is hard to stop. In writing this book I myself have noted that the practice of fiction becomes addictive and starts to grow on you, and you find yourself surprising yourself by inventing things you had not in mind to do. It is somewhat worrying.

"For all the time that you have not been asleep, I notice that you have not found the time to shave or comb your hair, or even to tie your shoelaces," says the *Rolling Stone* reporter dryly and with a note of disapproval.

The *Rolling Stone* reporter, incidentally, is dressed in a flared velvet lounge suit and silver boots, as befits one of his semi-bohemian calling.

"I had the time," yawns the villain carelessly, "but I preferred to spend it flicking ink pellets out of the window at strangers and making suggestive remarks to my chambermaid. To tell the truth, I have not even changed my underpants."

The *Rolling Stone* reporter is somewhat taken aback by this attitude, but the other two spies have long resigned themselves to the fact that in the first villain they are dealing with some dangerous character out of Dostoyevsky.

"Be that as it may," sneers the head villain, "while you others were indulging your bourgeois penchant for rest, I have been tirelessly plotting and scheming and indulging the brilliant but irregular fancies which come only to those lonely souls who are brother to owl and sister to bat. And I have worked out," he concludes triumphantly, "how we may track down this Orbison fellow."

"And how is that, pray?" the others inquire politely.

The villain places a large tome on the table, fruit of his nocturnal cogitation.

"The phone book," he says.

"Also . . . ," breathe the others.

To be continued . . .

Chapter 31

"But what," says the second villain, "if Orbison has gone ex-directory? He may have lost touch with his fan base and become some snooty recluse who records sprawling three-hour experimental albums and plays croquet with the crowned heads of Europe."

"It is not so," says the *Rolling Stone* reporter. "His last single was a taut and workmanlike exposition of a classic pop sensibility filtered through a balls-out blue-collar rock attitude. He will be listed in the phone book. I take back my aspersions on your personal lifestyle," he says to the chief spy. "Sleepless, unshaven, boorish and unfragrant you may be, but there is no one I would rather have by my side in the trenches of rock journalism."

In his assumed role as journalist the chief spy nods his acknowledgment of the compliment and bashfully mumbles self-deprecating remarks. "Really, it might have occurred to any of you," he says flicking through the phone book. "Now let us see. Orbheimat . . . Orbheissen . . . Orbison D, Orbison G, Orbison P, Orbison, R, Esq.! Now we have him . . . "

They laugh triumphantly and make to a phone box . . .

Meanwhile Roy, Jetta and I are on our way to seek the man who gave us the briefcase. We intend to start from the last place we saw him and work from there.

But as we near Roy's house, from within comes the sound of his phone ringing.

"*Ach*," says Roy, "my phone is ringing, and as ill luck would have it I am outside the house."

"Do you happen to have your door key with you?" I say casually, fingering an inside pocket.

"Fortunately I do."

"Yes, that is fortunate," I say neutrally, studiedly primping Jetta's claws.

Roy lets himself into his house and courteously bids me enter. We go into the living room and he answers the phone.

"Here is R. Orbison," he says.

"Good day, Mr. Orbison," says the chief villain smoothly. I, as the novelist, cannot help knowing this, and yet I in the story hear it only as an indistinct burbling I politely try not to listen to.

"How may I help you?" inquires Roy.

"I represent a small consortium of journalists who wish to interview you," lies the baddie. "Among our number we represent such influential organs as the *Düsseldorf Zeitung* and *Rolling Stone* magazine. Would you be interested in an informal question and answer session regarding your new tour, or have you become the sort of snooty recluse who will only talk to the crowned heads of Europe?"

"I have no contempt for the humble foot soldiers of the Fourth Estate," says Roy. "I am happy to grant you an audience."

"Capital," says the spy. "Perhaps we should arrange a venue. Would you agree to meet me on a sinister patch of deserted waste ground at midnight?"

"I would not," says Roy. "For one thing, that is past my habitual bedtime. For another, I am proud to say you will not find any patches of deserted waste ground within Düsseldorf."

"*Hmm*," says the villain. "I was hoping for somewhere quiet and secluded without witnesses—I mean, unaccredited journalists. I have another suggestion. Do you know the Shady Loser Coffee Bar in the scary part of town?"

"I do not," says Roy, "but I do not like the sound of it."

"The place is somewhat raffish and bohemian in aspect but nowhere I would be ashamed to take my mother." He sniggers to himself as he says this, for although it is not technically untrue, what he neglects to say is that his mother is an evil cutthroat and forger of supermarket discount coupons.

"Very well," says Roy, "if the fates do not conspire against us we will rendezvous there in an hour."

"Will you be alone and unarmed?" inquires the spy smoothly. "I have a reason for asking."

"I will be accompanied by my good friend Ulrich Haarbürste and his terrapin Jetta," says Roy. "And just because I am from North America originally does not mean I carry guns everywhere. My music is my weapon—and my shield."

"Oh, now I'm really scared," says the villain sarcastically.

"I beg your pardon?" says Roy.

"I said nothing, perhaps the operator was startled by a mouse," says the deceiver easily. "I will hope to see you soon then."

He hangs up and turns to his confederates. "Success! Orbison has agreed to meet us."

"Capital!" says the *Rolling Stone* reporter. "You talked quite some time already. Did you obtain any interesting biographical details or quotable quotes from him?"

"Yes, it turns out he <u>is</u> from North America originally, and he said that his music is his weapon—and his shield."

"Also," says the *Rolling Stone* man, scribbling in his notebook. "I am impressed. This is more than we have discovered about Orbison in many years. You are a dab hand at the obtaining of information."

"You should see me when I am equipped with a dark cupboard and some unruly earwigs. . ." the villain mutters darkly.

"I am sorry, what was that?"

"Nothing, I was mumbling bashful words of self-deprecation," lies the bad man smoothly.

"I guarantee you," he continues, "that by the time we have finished with Orbison, there will be no point in anyone else interviewing him ever again!!!"

He winks at his true confederates and they snigger nastily and rub their hands with glee. . .

TO BE CONTINUED! In the next chapter.

Chapter 32

"Capital," says Roy, putting down the phone. "I have been given the means of making amends with the *Rolling Stone* reporter and getting back in touch with my fan base." Briefly he recounts the salient points of the phone call. "I would be glad if you would accompany me."

"Of course, Roy."

"Press conferences make me nervous. If the strain becomes too much I will make a gesture with my handkerchief thus." He takes out his handkerchief and flourishes it in a certain way which I mark well. "Upon this signal you must stand up and say that you have had a premonition of a disaster threatening us all and that we must abandon the conference and flee the building."

"Very well," I say. "Perhaps, to make that more convincing, I should at the same time take some action to. . .cover and protect you in some way?" My hand twitches toward my inner pocket.

"Do as you think fit."

In the front hall Roy picks up the briefcase the man gave him but then pauses and reflects. "I had hoped to kill two birds with one stone but finding the owner of the briefcase will have to wait for now. I do not care to take it into a place with such a disreputable name."

He puts the briefcase down and we make to the bus stop.

Punctually we arrive at the Shady Loser Coffee Bar. It is that very same cafe in the scary part of town which we passed the night before. At this earlier hour it does not look quite so bad and we see no one more scary than a couple of failed car designers sitting in a corner looking sad. It is nonetheless not a place one would care to take one's mother or immediate superior at work unless they were an evil cut-throat or tax evader.

We look around for the *Rolling Stone* reporter or anyone with a notebook and the air of eager boyish inquiry that denotes a journalist but see no one.

However, a waiter bows to Roy and says, "You are expected in the back room."

There is a seedy back room to the cafe which is rented out, no questions asked, to parties of wild-eyed students who wish to secretly debate VAT reform or agitate for more cycle lanes. Today the chief villain has reserved it for his so-called press conference. We knock and enter.

The four men who greet our eyes look little like journalists, apart from the *Rolling Stone* reporter in his trademark flared velvet trousers and silver platform boots and silver afro wig.

However, they all carry notebooks and sharpened pencils, so we suspect nothing. We do not recognize Otto as the one who gave Roy the briefcase, as he has changed his beard.

"Mr. Orbison, welcome!" says the head villain with a big false smile. Right away I can tell there is something wrong about this fellow but I cannot put my finger on what. Perhaps it is something about the Mexican bandit sombrero he wears or the bandolier of bullets around his chest. Nevertheless we have no reason to be suspicious, so we exchange handshakes and bows. "Thank you for your time. I hope you will find the arrangements satisfactory."

Some chairs have been arranged, two at a table for Roy and me (along with a cushion for Jetta) and four in a row facing us at a respectful distance across the room.

"This is quite satisfactory," says Roy as we sit. "Perhaps we should establish some ground rules. First, you will ask questions one at a time, raising your hands when you do so, so that I may see who is talking. Second, questions about me and Queen Elizabeth are out of bounds. We are just good friends. Third, please take note of Mr. Haarbürste, my . . . security adviser and personal psychic. If he has any sudden untoward premonitions the conference will be over and I advise you to run fast and take your belongings with you."

"Also," says the villain known as Otto. "A psychic? Have you ever appeared on 'Spooky Occurrences' or met Greta Sonderbar? I am a big fan of hers."

I decide to venture a little joke. "I have not," I say, "but I knew you were going to say that!"

"Christ," mutters the villain, turning pale and making the sign of the cross.

"Then if you will take your seats," says Roy.

They rush to do so and the press conference begins . . .

What can transpire? Only the next chapter shall reveal that.

Chapter 33

"You may commence," says Roy.

And so the press conference commences.

The lead villain is the first to hold his hand in the air.

"Heinrich Schmidt, *Düsseldorf Zeitung*. Do you recommend my readers to come and hear your new concerts?"

"I do," says Roy, "for they represent great value for money. No less than twenty-three songs are performed with workmanlike precision. My new backing group are diligent fellows and have been drilled for maximum efficiency. I do not wish to speak boastfully, but not a wrong note has been played thus far."

The spy in black raises his hand.

"Lothar Schmidt, *Mönchengladbach After Hours*. Do you have any plans to play in Mönchengladbach in the foreseeable future?"

"No," says Roy sternly, "for Mönchengladbach is a sadly unsatisfactory town. Let them look to the mass transit arrangements for their concert venues and then petition me to play there."

Another hand is raised.

"Otto Schmidt, *Just Seventeen* magazine. When making out with girls, do you get alarmed if the girl is the first to use her tongue?"

"It depends what she does with it," says Roy wryly.

Diffidently I say, "I cannot help noticing that you are all three called Schmidt. Are you perchance related, or is this a case for Greta Sonderbar, fearless girl reporter of 'Spooky Occurrences'?"

"As it happens, we are related," lies the first spy glibly. I as the narrator know that he is lying but I in the story do not. "It is quite a heartwarming tale. We are three brothers whose father dreamed of being a journalist but was prevented from doing so by a malevolent cabal of shadowy enemies who put it about that he was cavalier with the use of umlauts. He died a broken and pitiful man but we are each in our own way striving to avenge him by living out his dream."

He nudges the other two villains and they agree, "Yes, it is so, he speaks the truth."

He is a glib and plausible liar but something about his story rings alarm bells.

"What was your father's name?" I ask.

"Schmidt, naturally."

"Naturally."

"If I may venture a question—" says the *Rolling Stone* reporter.

"*Ooh*, but I have a good one," says the chief villain rudely, not even holding his hand in the air. "Do you have any plans to work with George Harrison again?"

"There are no plans but I would certainly like to," says Roy. "It depends when he is next in town. He spends most of his time in Bremen nowadays."

Stealthily I mutter, "It strikes me that that question came close to being too personal. Shall I end the press conference and initiate the emergency protocol?" My hand strays toward an inner pocket.

"No," murmurs Roy, "I can handle this."

Raising his hippy-bangle-covered hand, the *Rolling Stone* reporter says, "If I may be permitted. What kind of plectrum—"

"But I have a better one!" cries Lothar, riding roughshod over him. "What are your thoughts on the European Bank's interest rates?"

"They did not consult me when establishing the European Bank," says Roy wryly. "They may sort out their own messes now."

"I have a really interesting question," says the *Rolling Stone* reporter, pouting somewhat and holding his hand very high in the air.

But the three villains have been confabulating together in whispers and nudging one another. Suddenly the spy in the sombrero stands upright so that his hand is even higher than that of the *Rolling Stone* reporter and says, "Ah, but I have an even more interesting one! Has Mr. Orbison ever been given any unexpected presents by ordinary members of the public?"

"On occasion," grants Roy. "For example, I was once presented with a cream cake in the shape of a guitar by the Burgomeister of Potsdam."

"My, how interesting," says the fake reporter. Something about the sarcastic exaggeration of his tone strikes a false note.

Diffidently I say, "I cannot help noticing that you are wearing a sombrero and bandolier of bullets. Have you ever been a Mexican bandit?"

"As it happens I have lately had the privilege to ride with guerrilleros and known the savage thrill of burning people out of house and home, rustling donkeys, and cruelly pushing old ladies over so that they sit down heavily on cactuses—purely in a journalistic capacity, of course," he adds unctuously, with another false smile.

"Also," I say thoughtfully.

The *Rolling Stone* reporter is now standing on his chair with his hand very nearly brushing the ceiling in his eagerness to be heard. "If I may please be permitted to ask one question—" he says.

"I admonish you not to stand on chairs," says Roy. "People have to sit on them afterwards. Get down and await your turn."

Sadly the *Rolling Stone* reporter bows his head in acknowledgment of the rebuke and complies.

The three so-called Schmidt brothers have again been confabulating and sniggering villainously. The lead villain raises his hand and says, "In any case, I had not finished and have a follow-up question. May I inquire, has Mr. Orbison ever been unexpectedly given a briefcase in somewhat mysterious circumstances? I have a reason for asking."

"As it happens, I have," says Roy.

"And may I further ask, did Mr. Orbison at any point happen to look inside that briefcase, become alarmed at what he found, and contact the authorities? Again, I have a personal interest in the answer."

"I did not," says Roy.

"Aha!" cries the man in the sombrero while his two cohorts nudge each other.

The *Rolling Stone* reporter stands and bows and says, "With all due respect, I insist upon being allowed to ask a question."

"I am afraid," says the chief villain in tones of silken menace, "that I have decided to make this interview a *Düsseldorf Zeitung* exclusive."

And before our disbelieving eyes he takes out a gun!

He does not shoot the *Rolling Stone* man with it but hits him brutally on the top of his silver afro wig, and he drops unconscious to the ground and begins to snore.

Meanwhile the other two villains also take out weapons, a bread knife and a bomb respectively.

"I have heard of circulation wars," mutters Roy wryly, "but this is ridiculous . . . I think I will put an end to this press conference."

He takes out his handkerchief and flourishes it in a certain way.

I recognize my cue and stand and loudly say, "Roy, I have had a psychic premonition of disaster. There is great danger here. We must leave at once."

"Unglaublich," mutters the villain with the bomb, backing away from me and crossing his fingers superstitiously.

"Your psychic is quite correct," says the chief villain silkily, pointing the gun at Roy. "You are in great danger here. But I regret to inform you, you will not be leaving . . ."

To be continued!

Chapter 34

Now here is a pretty pickle! What can befall?

Read on if you dare . . .

The three villains advance on us, cocking their pistol, sharpening their bread knife and holding a lighted match near the fuse of their bomb.

"Where is the briefcase you were given last night?" hisses the spy in the sombrero. "If you do not return it to us you will be killed."

"You said they must be killed anyway," points out Otto.

"Yes, that is so," concedes Heinrich. "You must tell us where the briefcase is and then be killed."

"I will not tell you," says Roy. "You are a scoundrel of some sort and up to no good. I suspect the case did not belong to you in the first place."

"We . . . found it somewhere," says Heinrich slyly. "We are looking after it for the rightful owners."

He nudges his confederates and they chorus, "Yes, it is so."

"I am looking after it now," says Roy defiantly, "and it is somewhere safe where you will never find it again!"

"*Pah*," sneers the spy, "I will wager you have merely dumped it in your front hall."

Roy and I nonchalantly study our fingernails and pick bits of lint off Jetta.

The spy scowls. "Tell me where it is or things will go badly with you."

"I will not do so," says Roy.

"Then you leave me with no alternative," says the spy in tones of silken menace. "You are about to undergo a very unpleasant experience."

I cough diffidently and say, "Perhaps my terrapin might be spared this ordeal? You may be a bandit and cutthroat but I am sure you are too big a man to take it out on her."

"On the contrary," says the villain in tones of icy malice, "only last week I ran a steamroller over a duck whose owner had thwarted me in a scheme worth only five euros."

Such villainy! I shiver and clutch Jetta closer to me. Jetta for her part shrinks back into her carapace some way.

"Very well," I say, "but I warn you we shall try to escape. Perhaps you had better tie us up? If you have forgotten the rope I may be able to improvise . . . somehow . . ."

"We have no need of rope," sneers the criminal in tones of suave cruelty. "If you try to escape you will be variously shot, sawn and blown up." The villains brandish their various weapons menacingly.

"There seems no choice but to cooperate," mutters Roy.

"At least they have not confiscated my clingfilm," I say stealthily.

Meanwhile the three villains are confabulating about what to do with us.

"I have the perfect place nearby," says the leader . . .

What is that place? And what dark deeds can befall there? But will there be a silvery yet translucent lining at long last? Only a fool would rush in to the next chapter without considering the matter first.

Chapter 35

Roy, Jetta and I are marched at gunpoint (to say nothing of bomb and bread-knife point) out of the back door and across an alley and into a seedy lodging house.

As we are forced up several flights of a rickety staircase with an unpolished and splintery bannister and a dangerous rug we pass various degraded figures who swill cough medicine or play with yo-yos in an unsafe and intimidating manner or offer to sell us unsuitable pension schemes.

For reassurance I grip Jetta with one hand and a roll of clingfilm in an inner pocket with another.

On the third floor we pass through a door without knocking and find ourselves in an exceptionally dirty flat. The villains do not even wipe their feet upon entering, and I do not really blame them, for the floor is even filthier than the hall outside and indeed the doormat itself is a dead badger. A degraded and vicious-looking old crone is stirring an unhygienic-looking vat of soup on a dangerous-looking stove, muttering seditious sentiments to herself as she does so.

The woman turns and scowls. "My son!" she says in surprise.

"Gentlemen," says the spy in the sombrero, "my mother!"

Roy and I and the other two spies bow politely and the son and the mother embrace each other. Very touching, you might think— but you would be wrong. For while they are hugging the mother picks the son's pockets and the son steals his mother's bra, to give as a present to one of his floozies.

"What brings you here?" she inquires. "It cannot just be a social call to your old degraded mother, for you are evil."

"I am attending to villainy," he explains. "These are my prisoners."

Roy and I bow again. Roy says, "I am sorry to hear about the cabal of enemies who thwarted your husband's journalistic ambitions, Mrs. Schmidt."

The woman scowls. "I have no idea what you mean. My name is not Schmidt and my husband was a wicked desperado and semi-professional chicken-choker."

She turns and dips one of her filthy fingerless mittens into the vat of soup and then licks her hand.

"You are just in time, son," she says. "This foul and unhealthy soup is as ready as it will ever be. I have spat in it for extra flavor, the way I used to when you were an urchin."

"Ah Mutti, that brings back memories, but I do not have time to sample your degraded cooking. Time waits for no man and business is afoot."

"Is there a lot of money involved?" says the crone with a sly cackle.

"Yes, but I will not give you any of it," he laughs. "And if you come begging I will punch you."

Such infamy!

The crone laughs too. "That's my boy! I raised you well."

"According to our perverted values, you certainly did."

The other two spies are quietly shocked at this behavior but say nothing.

"I need to use the attic," says Heinrich. "I trust you have intimidated the neighbors and that if they hear any whimpers and moaning emanating from here they will raise no alarms?"

"The neighbors will not notice. They spend all their time whimpering and moaning themselves as they reflect on their poor career choices and the unstable property values in this neighborhood."

"Capital. There is one other thing. I trust this kitchen is infested with earwigs?"

"But of course, for my slovenliness is proverbial. In fact I have collected a jar of them, to put in the soup for extra protein, the way I used to when you were a villainous child with hair sprouting in ugly places."

The villain smiles. "I am afraid I have another use for your earwigs, mother, and if you object I will bludgeon you."

"I do not object," says his mother. "The fact is, I find earwigs hard to chew anyway, as my teeth are all rotten as I never brush them. I will put some spiders in the soup instead."

"Very good, although be assured that if you had objected, I would have bludgeoned you, and flushed your head in the toilet."

"That you would not," says the crone defiantly, "for the toilet never flushes—not that I would bother to flush it if it did!"

The mother and son laugh loudly at this. "A man never had a finer mother," the rogue opines. He gives her a rough hug, although in doing so he steals her hearing aid to sell on the internet.

Reader, I blanch. Yet his villainy must be established if what follows next is to be plausible.

"You two, upstairs," he says roughly, gesturing with his gun. Roy and I bow farewell to his mother and are marched up a wooden staircase to a dim-lit attic room with a dusty window.

The room is empty, apart from a cupboard.

"This is your last chance," he says. "Will you tell me where the briefcase is?"

"I will not do so," says Roy.

"Nor I," say I.

Jetta merely looks at him contemptuously.

"Then you have only yourselves and me to blame for what happens next," he hisses.

With a savage gesture he throws open the cupboard doors.

"Gentlemen," he cries, "meet my cupboard! You are about to become very, very familiar with it."

Roughly we are ushered inside.

"You will be locked in that darkened cupboard for quite some time. But do not think," he adds in tones of silken menace, "that I would be so cruel as to leave you in there alone." He is being ironic. "For the fact is, you will have some earwigs to keep you company!"

And he pours the jar of unruly earwigs into the cupboard with us.

"Goodbye for now," he says.

"Goodbye," we reply.

And then the door is shut and we are left alone in the dark—with the earwigs. . .

To be continued!

Chapter 36

Only a fool can fail to remember that Roy, Jetta and I have been shut in a darkened cupboard containing earwigs.

We hear the key being turned in the lock and the sound of the villain's footsteps receding downstairs.

Is it an illusion, or can we also hear the minute sounds of earwigs scurrying and slobbering?

We swallow nervously.

"This is a pretty kettle of fish," says Roy.

"Yes," I say. "The darkened cupboard aspect is not so bad, since all three of us are together to raise each other's spirits, but I confess to having an aversion to earwigs."

"Who does not?" asks Roy. "They are charmless and scurrying and have redundant numbers of legs, and, if the wildlife segment of *Guten Abend Düsseldorf* is to be relied upon, their personal habits would shame a Bavarian."

Roy suddenly stifles a moan.

"What is it?" I ask.

"I believe one just scurried over my shoe."

"Let us hope they stop there."

"I fear they will stop at nothing," says Roy. "An earwig is no respecter of persons."

"It is so."

"Just so long as they do not get into my pockets. I do not think I could stand it if earwigs crawled into my pockets."

The very thought makes me repress a whimper.

Roy says, "If there was only some way to protect ourselves from this menace."

"If only," I agree.

"If we could improvise some tight-fitting protective covering somehow."

"Yes, something of that nature would meet the case," I say.

"Can you think of any substance we could use in that way?"

"I regret I cannot."

Roy clears his throat.

"I don't suppose . . . that is . . . do you happen to have any clingfilm about your person?"

A light dawns.

I strive to be nonchalant and keep the excitement out of my voice.

"As it happens, I believe I do. To be sure, I will check my pockets."
I do so. "Why, yes, Roy, it turns out I did bring a roll of clingfilm or
so with me."

"Also," says Roy. He waits expectantly—but two can play at that
game . . .

"Does that . . . suggest nothing to you?" he says hesitantly after
a while.

"What manner of thing, Roy?"

"The juxtaposition of need and supply. We need to be covered
in some convenient substance in order to protect our pockets and
sundry crevices from the ravages of the earwigs. As it turns out, we
are supplied with clingfilm."

"I am afraid I do not quite follow," I say airily.

There is a pause.

Roy clears his throat again.

"I was thinking, perhaps . . . the clingfilm might serve as such a
covering."

"Why Roy," I say, "are you asking me to completely wrap you in
clingfilm?"

"I believe I am," says Roy in a small bashful voice.

Though the circumstances are not what I would have chosen, this
is a great day indeed.

I decide to be pettish.

"But Roy," I say, "I thought you never wanted clingfilm to be so
much as mentioned again."

"I have changed my mind," says Roy. "I admit I spoke hastily and
in error. Clingfilm is an improbably useful substance and I regret
ever having maligned it."

I bow my acceptance of his apology, a useless gesture as the
cupboard is dark, and I bang my head on the door.

"Also," I say. "At your specific request, I will wrap you in clingfilm."

"Commence," says Roy.

With fumbling hands I take the clingfilm from my pocket. My heart beats faster as I hear the little sticky rasp as I start to unspool it. I start at the shoes and work my way up. Wrapping in the dark is strange but unexpectedly sensual. I wrap tightly and snugly, protecting him from all harm, paying special attention to the pocket areas. Soon, Roy Orbison is completely wrapped in clingfilm, in the dark but at his own request. My chakras explode with a shockwave of ecstasy.

"I cannot see you," I say, "but my questing fingertips tell me you are completely wrapped in clingfilm. At your own suggestion, I might add."

Roy makes a muffled sound that may be "Capital."

I wrap myself in clingfilm as best I can and we commence to stand in the dark. Since childhood I have had a fear of cupboards but I have to admit it is quite snug and cozy with Roy standing there by my side and Jetta within call. So as to make the ordeal more pleasant we make topical small talk and hum little tunes.

This may be an unusually happy point at which to end the chapter.

Chapter 37

Presently we hear footsteps ascending the stairs.

"Someone is coming," I say. "I had better remove the clingfilm."

Roy makes a noise that may be a grunt of assent.

Quickly I burst free of my clingfilm and force myself to remove it from Roy. I find it is not so difficult to do this, as I cannot see what I am doing.

The cupboard door is opened and the chief villain glares at us.

"Well?" he says. "Are you ready to talk yet?"

"We are not," says Roy. "We are made of sterner stuff than that."

"Bah!" says the villain. "I will lock you in for longer this time. I vow you will break in the end."

"Do your worst," says Roy with a merry nudge to me. "We are protected on our side by something that is strong and will not break."

"Yes," I say, "although it will tear off easily if you want it to."

Roy and I snigger to ourselves.

"I do not understand the joke," says the villain, feeling left out. He slams the door shut and locks it again.

We hear him stamping off in high dudgeon.

"Quick," says Roy, "into the clingfilm again before the earwigs get us."

Hurriedly I wrap Roy in clingfilm again, although not so hurriedly that I am without due reverence for this miracle that I have once more been granted. I start at the shoes and work my way up. Dark though it is, my questing fingers are now familiar with every inch of his clothing. I am like some blind tailor fashioning an outfit for an invisible man in an extremely confined space in some allusive and heartwarming fable. Soon, Roy Orbison is again completely covered in clingfilm. My intoxication is phenomenal.

"You are completely wrapped in clingfilm," I report. "You could now be stricken with a biblical plague of insects and not be inconvenienced."

Roy makes a noise I suspect is "Danke Schön."

Again I contrive to wrap myself as best I can manage and the pair of us stand and wait out our confinement insouciantly. I have left my mouth free and to pass the time I describe my plans for redecorating Jetta's bedroom while Roy makes noises of interest or surprise.

Presently I hear a sound of villainous boots clumping up the stairs again. Hurriedly but reluctantly I snatch the clingfilm from myself and Roy and by the time the villain opens the door we are nonchalantly whistling and studying our fingernails.

"What?" cries the chief villain in disbelief. "Not blubbering and whimpering yet? You must be men of stone!"

"Stone," says Roy laconically, "and a certain other substance . . . "

We smile knowingly, to the villain's annoyance.

"You are only prolonging the discomfort," hisses the villain. "Time is of no matter to me. I for my part am ensconced comfortably in the kitchen gambling and have already won most of my mother's gold teeth and one of her kidneys. You can stay here for the rest of the day and if necessary all of the night, and with no supper." He makes to close the door.

I nudge Roy to apprise him I am attempting a stratagem and say, "Really, it is not so bad in here. The fact is, since we cannot see the earwigs we have no fear of them. Now if you had been cruel enough to put a light in the cupboard, I do not think we could have stood it."

"It is so," agrees Roy.

"Aha!" cries the villain. "You have a large mouth, you blockhead, for now you have shown me how I may break you! The way is plain. I will put a candle in the cupboard so that you may see my many-legged henchmen milling about your shoes."

And without further ado he locates a stub of candle and lights it and places it by our feet!

Once more the cupboard door closes . . .

Chapter 38

"That was a piece of chicanery worthy of Machiavelli," says Roy in admiration once the villain has departed. "If you ever ran for the town council you could rule Düsseldorf like a puppet master."

"I have sometimes thought so," I admit. "However, I have not yet decided upon a political program, apart from equal rights for terrapins and the installation of a splendid monument in the town square depicting . . . a certain person wrapped in a . . . certain substance." I cough nervously. "Be that as it may, I have to say that my cleverness has backfired somewhat on this occasion. For it seems to me that the earwigs *are* more scary now we can see them!"

"It is so," says Roy. "I do not care for the monstrous and distorted shadows the flickering candlelight throws from them. Let us enclingfilm ourselves once more with all haste."

"By all means," I say.

Once more I start at the shoes and work my way up. It is even more enjoyable now that I can see and admire my work. It is rather romantic wrapping by candlelight and the clingfilm reflects a delightful ruddy glow. I am like some playful Loki encircling Brünnhilde with his protecting fire in some extremely small-scale production of the Ring Cycle for agoraphobics. Soon Roy is once again completely wrapped in clingfilm. My every nerve ending tremors and bursts into song.

"You are completely wrapped in clingfilm," I say. "The earwig who can pass through that will be worthy of your pockets."

We settle down to a comfortable talk and hum.

All too soon, however, there again comes the sound of the villain ascending the stairs. Regretfully I divest Roy of his clingfilm cocoon once more.

"This time see if you can con him out of a pumpernickel sandwich," says Roy as we hide the remnants of clingfilm. "I confess the thought of going without food all day grieves me."

The villain unlocks the door and flings it open dramatically.

"This is your last chance to talk," he says evilly.

"We will not do so," says Roy. "Unless you mean topical small talk," he adds wryly with a merry bravado.

"I do not," says the villain. "In the sorry netherworld of villainy we take no interest in topical matters of the day, apart from the movements of large sums of money and tales of people who have been maimed or injured in amusing ways. I was referring to the briefcase."

"Then we have nothing to say to you."

"Then I will be forced to—oh, but there is a thread loose on your jacket, look—allow me." He makes as if to pick a loose thread off Roy's dark clothing—but it is a trick! For there is no thread and at the last minute his hand darts inside Roy's jacket—and comes out with Roy's door key and his wallet!

"Aha!" he crows, waving them in our faces tauntingly. "Did your mother never warn you not to let strange men fix your clothes? My mother taught me the sly but nimble art of pick-pocketing!"

"Give those back," says Roy.

"I will not do so." He shamelessly riffles through Roy's wallet until he finds a library card with his address on it. "Now I have your address and the means of entrance to your house! Upon reflection I am convinced you have merely dumped the briefcase in your front hall and I will now be going there to check!"

Roy's eyes are unreadable behind his dark glasses. "Do what you have to," he says flatly. "But I warn you if you do so you will be adding trespass and burglary to the list of your crimes."

"I am proud to say that every crime from the theft of bank pens to the improper use of railway emergency cords is listed on my curriculum vitae! Moreover if I do find the briefcase I will then come back here and kill you!"

Cackling to himself, he shuts the door and we hear him clomping off.

"I am sorry, Roy," I say, "I forgot to ask for a sandwich."

"It is of no moment," says Roy. "I have other worries right now. I confess the thought of that oaf trespassing in my house leaves me bereft of appetite."

"Take heart," I say, "as the briefcase is in the front hall he will not stay long."

"And then he will be back to kill us! And even if we do escape death I will now have to cancel my library card, in case he misuses it, or takes out rude books in my name."

"That is true. However, just now we have a more immediate concern," I say. "For it seems to me the earwigs are massing to attack!"

"It is so," says Roy. "Make with the clingfilm with promptitude."

"I will do so," I say.

I loosen the film with a sticky rasp. . .

And suddenly the door is flung open again and the villain returns!

"Aha!" he cries. "I thought you were up to some mischief! I faked going downstairs by making receding clomping noises with my shoes—in reality I merely clomped over to a corner and held my breath! So! Clingfilm is your secret. Very well then," he says with silky menace. "It appears I have no option but to confiscate your clingfilm!"

What can happen now? Will he make good on his threat? Readers of a nervous disposition or those needing heart medication may want to skip the next chapter, which is horrific.

Chapter 39

If you do not remember the climax of the previous chapter it is either due to mental deficiency—or some self-defense mechanism of the brain protecting you from the distressing memory! But you will soon be reminded and I regret to announce that this chapter is even more horrible. If you feel faint you should lie down near an open window at once.

"Yes," recaps the villain, "I am going to confiscate your clingfilm, all the rolls of it! Hand it over now!"

He gestures with his revolver.

I look from the gun to my clingfilm and back again. At this range there is no way he can miss. My palms sweat. My mouth is dry. I wish to be far away, on some pleasant desert island where everyone is happy and there is a keen respect for property rights.

"I will not do so," I hear myself say in a small desolate voice. "You will not take my clingfilm."

"What was that?" roars the villain in disbelief.

"I said you will not take my clingfilm!" I say louder. "Shoot me if you will but I will still not give it to you. I estimate there can only be twenty or thirty bullets in that gun. You would have to shoot me many more times than that to make me hand over my clingfilm."

"So," says the villain, "a hero! I can almost respect you for that." He muses thoughtfully. "You and I are not so very different, you know. True, you are polite and well-behaved, and I like rolling marbles under the feet of nuns so they go flying in the air and I can see their knickers, but we each have our own integrity. Tell me, do you ever cross the street against the traffic light?"

"That would be the act of a fool," I say.

"A fool—or a man who is even braver than you!" The villain rubs his unshaven chin pensively. "Very well, then, Mr. Hero, perhaps I would be wasting my time shooting you—but how about if I shot your friend—or your terrapin!"

Sniggering horribly, he points the gun at Roy and then at Jetta and back again.

I turn pale.

"You may take my clingfilm," I say in a small faint voice.

Reluctantly I hand over the roll.

"Thank you," says the villain. "And now will you please to turn out your pockets."

I feel dizzy and the cupboard swims around me.

I swallow nervously. "I will do so," I say at last. I turn my trouser pockets inside out.

"Those are well-kept pockets, remarkably free of lint," says the villain in grudging admiration. "However, I was not referring to them. I meant your inner jacket pockets where I suspect you of harboring more clingfilm!"

I turn ashen and quiver. "You are a cruel man," I say, and reach into my inner pocket and take out a spare roll.

"Danke Schön," says the villain as he takes it. "And now the others."

"I assure you, there are no others!"

"In a long career of stealing everything from gold bullion to old ladies' half-sucked cough drops I have learned when someone is holding out on me! Give me the rest of your clingfilm or it will go badly with you!"

This time I think I really might pass out. With every nerve ending screaming in rebellion I force my arm back into my pocket and bring out another roll of clingfilm and mutely hand it to him. He makes an encouraging gesture with his gun and then aims it at Roy and I reluctantly produce one more.

"Your pockets are capacious," says the villain. "I believe I will have my tailor make me something similar the next time I am about to go stealing piglets. But I believe we have now reached the end of your little treasure trove . . . or have we?" He grins and prods with the gun. "I estimate there is yet one more roll of clingfilm in there! Hand it over or else!"

Who would blame me if I broke down completely at this point? If Roy and Jetta were not there it is possible I would weep hysterically and beg for clemency. As it is I cry, "You must not take my clingfilm!" and cower in the corner of the cupboard trembling. But the evil man is merciless and by a mixture of threats and brute force he succeeds in wrenching the last lonely roll of clingfilm from my pocket. I fall from the cupboard and collapse to the floor more dead than alive, a broken and pitiful man.

"So," he gloats. "Now your clingfilm is mine. I will sell it to a tinker and you will never see it again. But just to be sure . . . perhaps we should perform a body search." He hauls me to my feet.

"A body search?" I croak brokenly. "What can you hope to find? You have left me bereft of clingfilm, you monster in human shape."

But without remorse he proceeds to pat me down expertly.

"Aha!" he cries. "So I left you without clingfilm, did I? Then what, pray, is this?"

With a flourish he produces the emergency roll concealed up my sleeve. It is only a small one, consisting of a normal roll sawn in half so as to allow me to flex my arm, but he takes it nonetheless.

"I had forgotten about that," I say. "A sundry roll left over from my catering days. You will find no more."

"We shall see," he says. "Aha! And what is this I feel here?" Mercilessly he tears off my coat and lifts my shirt to reveal one more roll taped to my backbone.

"You must not take that!" I cry. "It is a spinal support. If you remove it I may collapse like a jellyfish."

"I do not care! Now, though, I believe you are finally relieved of all your clingfilm, every roll of it."

I hum nonchalantly and study my nails.

"Wait, though—it strikes me that the bottoms of your trousers are unusually baggy for one so otherwise dapper! Roll up your pants at once!"

"Please," I beg, "not the pants—surely you would not—"

"Do so at once or you will surely rue the day!"

It is the death knell. All hope is gone. All I can do is memorize the villain's face and pray for the day when he will stand in the dock and I from the witness stand will say, "That is the man who took my clingfilm."

Numbly I comply. I lift my trouser bottoms to reveal the emergency emergency rolls taped to my shins. Savagely he tears them from me. Now there are truly no more rolls left.

"That is it," I say hollowly, "there is no more."

However, he also makes me take off my shoes and discovers the loose clingfilm folded up into small flat packages concealed therein.

Roughly he places me back in the cupboard. For a moment I have a gleam of hope, but he even thinks to take the discarded remnants of clingfilm littering the floor from the previous wrappings.

"Farewell once more, gentlemen," he says.

"Farewell," we say, politely but disconsolately.

"This time you really are left to the tender mercies of my insects! There is no clingfilm to protect you now!" Sneering, he bends and cruelly flicks several of the earwigs on the bottom just to put them in a really foul mood. "Rest assured that this time I really am going away—there will be no one to hear your whimpers! I think, if I do find the briefcase, I will simply leave you here until they have eaten you!"

He slams the door shut and locks it and this time his shoes really do clump down the stairs.

"You have a surprising amount of clingfilm," says Roy thoughtfully.

"*Had*," I say in a sad small voice. Fortunately the villain did not find the small scrap of clingfilm kept wadded under my armpit. It is not nearly enough to begin to wrap Roy but I rub it against my cheek soothingly.

"And now what are we to do?"

"Be probed and nibbled by insects!" I say dismally.

For the earwigs are massing to attack . . .

To be continued . . . !

Chapter 40

I do not wish to speak immodestly, but I am pleasantly surprised by how good I am at cliff-hangers. I believe when I have finished this novel I will contrive to write a thrilling TV series.

Unfortunately I have noted before that clingfilm is hard to pick up on a video camera. I suppose they would resort to some fake stage clingfilm, but I would not be prepared to stoop to such a measure.

On the other hand perhaps I will write an opera.

So then. Recall if you dare that Roy and I and my terrapin Jetta were imprisoned in a cupboard at the mercy of a horde of enraged earwigs with no clingfilm to protect us.

In the flickering candlelight we can see our insecty enemies milling about our feet on their innumerable pairs of legs, their feelers wiggling obscenely as they prepare to invade our personal space.

Who can tell what they will do? At the very least they seem certain to scurry all over us and lick us in intimate places.

"Is it just me," I whisper, "or are there even more of them now than when we started?"

"Possibly they are breeding," says Roy. "I tell you they fornicate like three Swiss skiing instructors on top of a pile of Bavarian milkmaids."

We can only wait in horror for their attack. They seem certain to invade our pockets and even our socks.

"Perhaps I could—stamp on them?" I suggest.

"They would squash horribly under your shoe. Personally I would have to cut my foot off afterwards."

It is so. They are the perfect attack beasts in that their squelchy death would be even more horrible than their disgusting wriggly life. We cannot prevent them overrunning us. Bravely we steel ourselves for the onslaught but inside I am near breaking point. I reflect that if they do eat us it would almost be preferable to them merely nesting in us. I do not think I would wish to live with the memory of having had my pockets and various crevices infested with earwigs. A horrible thought comes to me—is their name a clue to their habits? Will they crawl into my very ears and take up residence there? The thought almost makes me pass out.

As I watch in horror, one crawls up to the tip of my shoes, wiggles its feelers, and then bustles away again.

"What are you waiting for, damn you?" I almost scream at it.

"They are toying with us, the brutes," opines Roy.

The tension is unbearable. All around us I seem to hear the scampering of tiny feet.

"I believe I can hear a chewing sound!" I suddenly cry.

"They must be nibbling my shoelaces," groans Roy. "I cannot bear to look."

Neither can I, but the sound continues, a small but relentless chomping noise. I commend my soul to God and bid a fond farewell to my shoes.

"Sweet Mother of Mercy, we are sunk without trace," laments Roy.

I can take the suspense no longer. I nerve myself to look down at our feet again, since to see what horror is taking place is better than guessing what they may be up to.

And then I see it—the miracle!

"Look, Roy!" I cry. "We are saved! Saved! Jetta! Jetta has saved us! Jetta is eating the earwigs!"

It is so! It is she who is chomping and slurping! My plucky terrapin has come to our rescue.

"Go, Jetta, go!" I cry. "Annihilate them all, my avenging angel!"

"Show no mercy, Jetta," says Roy.

And indeed she shows no mercy whatsoever to the earwigs. Relentlessly she cuts a swath through them, turning this way and that seeking whom she may devour, plodding inexorably through their ranks like some unstoppable dinosaur, her head darting and pouncing remorselessly, pausing in her rampage only to chew each mouthful thoroughly, as I have taught her.

Soon not an earwig is left alive within the bounds of the cupboard. Jetta nods slightly to herself in satisfaction and licks her lips.

Then she goes to sleep.

Roy and I let out huge sighs of relief.

"If I have any political pull in this town I will see to it that that plucky little terrapin receives a medal for this day's work," says Roy, with a quiver of suppressed emotion in his voice.

On this note of joy I will end the chapter.

Chapter 41

Unless you have corroded your brain with a sequence of late bedtimes, you will remember the heartwarming climax of the last chapter, where my terrapin Jetta fought like a tigress against a vast army of earwigs to defend me and Roy.

Nevertheless our predicament remains an unfortunate one. We are trapped in a cupboard with a prospect of almost certain death and no lunch. We are also horribly bereft of clingfilm.

Furthermore we are fast running out of topical small talk with which to make the ordeal more pleasant.

"I think I will use airplane wallpaper in Jetta's bedroom," I am finally reduced to saying.

"I do not give a _____ about Jetta's bedroom," says Roy in a rare lapse from his customary urbanity. "We must contrive an escape from this cupboard before the man comes back to kill us or I die of peckishness, whichever comes first."

"It is so," I admit.

"It is destructive, but perhaps we should seek to use our combined strength to attempt to burst forth from the confines of this cupboard."

"In the circumstances we would be within our rights to damage his property." I lower my voice. "But what if he has tricked us again and is once more lurking nearby ready to surprise us?"

"It is possible. I will put my eye to the keyhole and look for him." Roy stoops to bring his dark glasses next to the keyhole. "*Ach*," he says, "my view is occluded by the key."

"But if he has left the key in the lock then I believe I have a plan!" I take the last scrap of clingfilm I have been nursing, roll it up into a taut narrow length and double it so that it resembles a slender pair of pincers. I insert the tool I have fashioned into the keyhole and delicately clasp the key with it. After several attempts I am able to turn the key—a click is heard and we are freed!

Roy says, "I think I may have to write a song on my new album extolling the many virtues of clingfilm."

"If you will permit me, Roy, I have never presumed to suggest it, but I have long felt that a song about clingfilm is the one thing your oeuvre lacks."

We open the cupboard and step forth into the attic, holding each other's hands for courage in case the villain is still hiding there ready to pounce on us. But he is not there.

However, something else is!

"My clingfilm!" I gasp. "It has returned to me!" I sink to my knees in gratitude and joy, for the clingfilm is still there on the floor where he has negligently discarded it. There are all the rolls of it and I count them twice to be sure, giving each one a little welcome-home kiss as I stow them securely back in my various pockets and flaps, not forgetting the half a roll I keep up my sleeve for emergencies. "Now we are fully armed again," I say to Roy as I push this last back on to its homemade spring-loaded quick-release mechanism, which I copied off a Hollywood film about guns and floozies.

"However, the villains are better armed," says Roy, "and since the bloodlust has passed from Jetta we are outnumbered." The spy known as Heinrich has gone to burgle Roy's house, but from downstairs we can hear the sounds of the remaining two villains confabulating and gambling and the harsh cursing and unpleasant cough of his degraded mother.

"We must make plans to deal with them but they must not overhear us," whispers Roy.

We huddle in a corner and confer in low voices.

"Like it or not we must deal harshly with them or they will attempt to prevent our escape," says Roy. "I for one am prepared to use physical force."

"I also," I say. "But the villain's mother? No matter how degraded she is, it goes against every tenet of politeness to assault an old lady we have barely been introduced to."

"It is so," says Roy, rubbing his chin. "If we cannot reason with her we will have to shove her gently into a chair and hope she is so aged in the bones as to find rising again difficult."

"Very well."

"We must take them by surprise," says Roy. "If they have any warning of our coming they will attempt to variously saw and bomb us, and hell alone knows what that unhygienic mother will assay."

"Perhaps," I suggest, "if we were to don a disguise before descending, in order to put them off their guard for a few vital seconds?"

"I see no disguises here," says Roy.

"No," I say, "but we do have the clingfilm back." I presume to nudge him knowingly. "If you know what I mean."

"I do not," says Roy. "Please state the thing you mean."

"Can you have forgotten so soon the splendid costumes I wrought from it only last night, which won you first prize at the fancy dress party?" I try hard to keep any suggestion of sulkiness from my voice.

"*Ach so*," says Roy, "I am a clod and an ingrate. Then the way is plain. You will improvise disguises from clingfilm at once."

I consult with myself. "You know," I say, "it strikes me that at least one of those two villains was markedly superstitious. Perhaps we could take advantage of that . . . "

"There is no time for suggestive ellipsis," says Roy. "State your case plainly."

And I do so—whispering in his ear. Who do I not wish to hear me? Why, you, dear reader! For your heightened enjoyment you may not know what my plan is yet. For now you must just attempt to guess what it can involve.

"That plan is sound at bottom," says Roy a moment later. "Commence to wrap me in clingfilm at once."

I start at the feet and work my way up. I wrap carefully and thoughtfully. I am like some tender mother who has neglected to make a costume for her child's school nativity play until the last minute and so been forced to improvise one out of a certain household necessity and then realized that she is making the best damned costume ever and the child has never looked more beautiful and she wishes she could keep her child wrapped up in that household necessity for ever and ever and keep it locked safely in a room for the rest of its life so she could always look at it like that and cherish it forever but she knows that interfering killjoys from the social services would come and find the child eventually and institute complicated legal proceedings and besides she supposes the child would eventually become unhappy and odd so she has to let it go even though her heart is breaking but still it looks so damned beautiful she will never forget that moment in a thousand years. I do it with several layers but not too many, so that the wrapping is by no means opaque but has a faint silvery sheen in places and twinkles as with heavenly lights in others. As on the previous occasion when I made a costume, I wrap his arms and legs individually—in this case so that they are free to move so that he may thump the villains if we can put them off guard. Soon, Roy Orbison is completely costumed with clingfilm. If loving this is wrong I do not want to be right.

"You are completely wrapped with clingfilm," I mutter to myself thoughtfully in a fury of creation, "and yet I am not quite satisfied with the effect yet . . . "

And I proceed to make some further adjustments. What they are you may not know just now . . .

A few moments later I step back and consider. I am so pleased with the results that I start to think boastfully. I reflect that my inborn talent should be propagated for generations to come and resolve sometime soon to post an anonymous donation to a sperm bank. Then with more humility I realize that God put this fire in me and it is his to bestow or withhold at will.

"You are ingeniously disguised with clingfilm," I say. "Now let us see what will befall . . . "

Jetta wakes up and blinks in astonishment.

To be continued! Very soon.

Chapter 42

Downstairs the two junior villains and Heinrich's foul mother are playing cards for money. Practiced in deception, she is making good her losses to Heinrich and has won a kidney from Otto to replace the one her son has won from her.

"Oh *scheisse*," she curses as a new hand is dealt, "I cannot believe how bad these cards are. A three, a four, a forged library card that must have got shuffled up by mistake, and two other useless cards. I will never win with this hand."

Otto and Lothar cackle to themselves and shove large amounts of money into the pot, confident of victory.

"Oh, what the hell, I need the action," she says casually, and matches their bet.

They raise each other for a few rounds, markers and IOU notes taking the place of cash as the betting heats up. Then the old woman cackles and turns over her cards—to reveal three aces and two kings!

"Pontoon!" she cries. "I win again!"

"I see where Heinrich gets his lying technique from," says Otto ruefully.

"Now you owe me both your kidneys," the evil old woman cackles. "I will keep one and sell the other to whichever renal patient will perform the most sexual favors for me."

"Wait a minute," says Otto quizzically, "how can you have three aces when I had two myself?"

"And now I come to think of it I had three kings," says Lothar.

They exchange suspicious glances while the old woman hums and looks casual.

"She is cheating," says Otto, outraged.

"Seize her."

"Dangle her upside down."

"Confiscate her false teeth to ensure repayment of debts."

Perhaps fortunately, just then a distraction arrives—for Jetta and I come boldly down the stairs!

"What," cries Lothar, seizing his knife menacingly, "out of the cupboard? Return at once or it will go badly with you."

"The psychic!" cries Otto, paling. "There is something eerie about his escape. He has manipulated the cupboard doors in some uncanny fashion."

"Woe," I cry, "woe and calamity." I have a sad face.

"What has happened?" asks Lothar.

"Roy," I say, my voice a broken whisper, "Roy has expired from ill-usage. He is currently dead!"

I put my hand on my brow to express misery. Jetta for her part gets into the spirit of things by bowing her head sadly, or perhaps she is merely scanning the floor for more insects.

Otto and Lothar sit down heavily.

"Dead?" says Otto sadly. "But I only just met him."

"He seemed so nice," says Lothar.

"And in the best of health."

"Yes, it makes you think." They are plainly shaken.

"We had best call the coroner," says Otto.

"We will get into trouble for this."

"Fools!" cries the old woman. "Can you not see he is lying? I know an unpracticed bluffer when I see one. See how he blushes as he speaks!"

"I am not," I say, reddening even more. "It is merely hot in here."

"Bah, she is right," cries Otto angrily. "We are surrounded by cheats and mountebanks."

They advance on me angrily.

"Seize him."

"Punish him for lying."

"Wash his tongue with soap."

"Pull his ears and shake him roughly."

"Make him stand in a special corner for discredited liars."

Fortunately a further distraction arrives. . .

There are footsteps upon the stairs.

"I would like to inquire," says Otto silkily, taking up his bomb, "if Orbison is dead, then who, pray, is descending the stairs?"

"It is Roy's ghost," I say sepulchrally, and Roy appears, disguised as a ghost by the miracle of clingfilm.

The effect is uncanny, though I say so myself. I have affixed trailing streamers of clingfilm to each of his various limbs to give the appearance of some sort of spectral ectoplasm and wrought a clingfilm halo atop his head and at least a sketchy suggestion of a pair of angel wings on his back. The silvery sheen and glinting lights make him appear less a man than some eerie kind of phantom.

"*Whoooo*," says Roy, somewhat muffled.

Otto and Lothar turn pale and back away in terror, crossing themselves and attempting to remember prayers.

"By my psychic powers I have brought him here to haunt you," I say. "He is vexed with you for your ill-usage and unless you allow me and my terrapin to escape he will hound you without let until the end of your days. Your careers will stall, you will have no luck in gambling or pursuing floozies, your pension schemes will prove inadequate and wherever you move property values will depreciate due to his unearthly moaning."

"*Whoooo*," says Roy again, scarily.

"By all means escape," says Otto quickly. "Just take that spooky apparition with you." Lothar nods.

But the old woman is not deceived.

"*Pah*," she says contemptuously. "Fools and cowards! If that is a ghost then I am Greta Sonderbar of 'Spooky Occurrences,' intrepid girl ghost hunter and fearless exposer of charlatans and mountebanks!" And she stamps on Roy's foot, causing him to hop and say "Ouch."

"We have been taken in!" cries Otto angrily, preparing to light his bomb. But Roy has closed in by this point and with one swift blow he thumps Otto on the shoulder, causing him to cry with pain and drop his bomb!

But meanwhile Lothar waves his knife.

"You are unarmed and defenseless," he cackles nastily, brandishing it at me.

"Not quite," I say, and quick as a flash I activate the spring-loaded quick-release mechanism in the arm of my jacket and the sawn-off half-roll of clingfilm shoots out of my sleeve and pops into my hand and I brutally rap him on the knuckles with it so that he drops his knife and says "Ow."

"Good work," says Roy. I seize the knife and pick up the bomb while Roy punches the villains on the jaw so they are dazed and groggy.

But then we are confronted with the old woman, who is advancing toward us waving a greasy and unhygienic frying pan in one hand and a rusty bottle opener in another. She will variously bludgeon us or attempt to prize our extremities off unless she is prevented.

Guiltily we exchange a glance and then shove her down into a chair as gently as we can.

"Oh, you brutes, it will take me forever to lever my old bones out of this chair!" she cries, flailing pathetically.

Roy and I blush and look down at our feet in shame.

"We are sorry and will come round to perform household chores for you at some point in the future by way of making amends," says Roy.

Quickly we tie the villains up in chairs with tea towels and make a soothing cup of tea for the old woman.

The villains now look sheepish and forlorn.

"Please may I have my bomb back?" says Otto bashfully. "I was only issued it for the day and I will get in trouble at work."

"I am sorry, I must confiscate it for the time being," I say. "However, I will write you out a receipt for it. If you behave well you may have it back at some point in the future when all this has been resolved."

He bows and mumbles his thanks.

As Roy's arms are free I see to my regret that he is pulling the clingfilm from him himself.

We put some ice on the villains' bruises, write out a receipt for their weapons and leave at top speed.

Chapter 43

Trepidantly we venture forth into the degraded lodging house and descend the stairs.

On the next floor down we are accosted by ragged figures who cough and hold out their hands for alms.

"Please help me, kind sirs," says a piteous figure. "I was a trick-cyclist by trade, but one day performing in the park I made a mistake and ran over a small child's foot, causing her to cry and drop her ice cream. Since then I have been shamed and outcast."

"I for my part was a champion yo-yo performer," says another. "But one day showing off in the street I lost control of my implement and hit a relative of the mayor on the nose, causing him to bleed on his shirt. Since then all doors have been closed to me and I cannot bear to look at a yo-yo. I do not have an adequate pension scheme."

Roy takes pity and magnanimously scatters a handful of coins, which they crawl after shamelessly.

"I admit to having a fear of trick-cyclists and yo-yo artistes," I say.

"Who does not?" says Roy. "They are a menace to themselves and others. Moreover those are foolish careers with little stability and no future once arthritis sets in."

Shuddering, we descend to the next level, where behind closed doors failed car designers can be heard moaning and wringing their hands.

"Five wheels, what was I thinking?" cries one.

"The sooner we are out of here the gladder I will be," says Roy.

"I too," I say. "This is no place for respectable citizens or innocent terrapins." Jetta for her part has withdrawn her head very nearly into her shell and only her eyes and adorable little nose can be seen protruding. "At least we can congratulate ourselves on having escaped the villains' lair."

But just then a figure appears in the lobby below us—the lead villain, in his trademark Mexican bandit hat!

"Let this be a lesson to you not to congratulate yourself prematurely," says Roy dryly.

The chief villain is whistling a cheerful if nasty tune and looks pleased with himself—as well he might, for he is carrying the mysterious briefcase he must have burgled from Roy's house. We swallow nervously as we perceive his gun sticking out of his bandolier. He lingers in the lobby playing a nasty trick on the degraded wretches who cluster round him begging for alms—he throws his trick coin tied to a piece of thread onto the floor and then yanks it away from them as they crawl to grab it, chuckling loudly to himself at this unpleasant fun.

"What a rotten man," says Roy in outrage. "I confess I would love to put a spoke in his mysterious plans and return that briefcase to its rightful owner. But instead it seems more likely he will presently climb the stairs and shoot us to death with his gun."

"It is so," I agree dismally. We look around for a hiding place or way of escape but there is none.

However, then a plan occurs to me.

"We have one thing on our side," I say. "We managed to recover my clingfilm."

"It is so," says Roy, "and I will wager you will find a means to extricate us from our predicament using that improbably useful miracle of science—although what that means could possibly be completely eludes me."

"There is one thing we might try," I say. And I lean forward and whisper in his ear. Again you may not know what I say! You may be hurt to feel excluded, but for now I am again concealing my plan for your heightened suspense and enjoyment.

"Also," says Roy, "that plan is completely logical and eminently sensible. You will proceed to wrap me in clingfilm in the manner you describe at once."

I bow. "As you wish, Roy."

I start from the feet and work my way up. I work hurriedly and fearfully and yet not without pride in craftsmanship and by no means without unbearable exhilaration. Though time is of the essence I cannot help but take a moment or two to admire the soft play of light on the pellucid miracle of science as I apply it to Roy's dark contours. Soon, Roy Orbison is completely wrapped in clingfilm. I am a cup filled with euphoria sitting on a saucer of gladness.

"You are completely wrapped in clingfilm," I comment. "But now I must proceed to the next part—to wrap you some more!"

You may not know yet exactly how I wrap him! But suffice it to say my plan involves wrapping Roy again and again and again, many many times, to a depth of many many layers. So much so that it involves using up all my remaining clingfilm! Soon the landing is littered with empty tubes and tears of joy are coursing down my features and ticking like little raindrops of happiness onto the floorboards. I am as weak as a kitten and happy as a cow.

"You are wrapped in clingfilm to a depth of many, many layers, in a manner that has used up all my remaining clingfilm," I finally gasp.

Roy makes sounds I cannot really hear at all, but by dint of much straining and diligent attention I finally surmise they may be "Capital, proceed with the next stage of the plan."

"Oh yes—the plan," I remember with a sudden start of recollection.

Some moments pass in hurried preparation . . .

Down in the lobby the villain finally tires of his mean game and allows one of the beggars to catch the coin. The poor man clutches it happily, crying, "At last, now I can invest in an adequate pension scheme," whereupon the villain cruelly yanks it out of his grasp and puts it back in his pocket with a big laugh. Sighing to himself, he starts to mount the staircase—and sees me and Jetta at the top of the first flight of steps!

"So," he cries, whipping out his gun, "the man with the well-groomed terrapin! I deduce you have managed to escape from my inefficient henchmen."

"It is so," I admit, "although you should not upbraid them for it, for they tried their best."

"Where is your friend who dresses in black?"

"Nowhere," I am forced to fib. "I have not seen him." Actually he is very close at hand.

"*Hmm*," says the villain suspiciously. "What is that behind your back?"

"Nothing," I again lie, blushing somewhat, "a trick of the shadows."

"I spend much of my working life lurking in shadows," he says silkily, "and I have never before seen a trick of the shadows resembling a large mass of a futuristic plastic-like substance that glints mischievously."

I hum noncommittally and examine my fingernails and flick bits of lint off Jetta.

The villain shrugs. "It does not matter. I will now shoot you many times for daring to escape. Farewell, Mr. Hero!"

"Farewell," I say, with a somewhat perfunctory bow.

"Always so courteous and correct," he sneers. "Where does it get you? What fun do you have? I almost pity you. You will die without having known the savage thrill of crawling under tables and tying people's shoelaces together or flicking meatballs across crowded restaurants into people's soup so their shirtfronts are splashed or sticking rude post-it notes on clergymen's backsides or swapping old ladies' handbags for trick ones that huge rubber snakes come out of or setting fire to badgers' tails and letting them loose in women's department store changing rooms so the women run out screaming and you can see their bras."

"With all due respect," I say defiantly, "you will go to prison without having known the happiness that comes of being nice and considerate to those around you."

"Bah," cries the villain, "prepare to be shot in the organs a hundred times or more!" And he starts to mount the stairs.

Briskly I step to one side, revealing that which is behind me. It is a huge ball of clingfilm at the center of which is a man-shaped figure in black.

"Prepare to be bowled over by Mr. Roy Orbison, completely wrapped in clingfilm!" I cry. And I give a big push and launch the ball of clingfilm and Roy down the stairs.

The villain's eyes widen in alarm as he sees Roy rolling down toward him, gathering speed as he goes. "No!" he cries, but then the ball/Roy is upon him and he is knocked over and flattened.

To my alarm Roy bounces off a wall and crashes through the apartment house doors and goes rolling down the street a way, but the derelict who caught the trick coin helps me retrieve him. I then watch helplessly as the derelict takes a rusty penknife and releases Roy from the clingfilm ball.

"Thank you, my man," says Roy to the degraded figure as he helps him out. "Tell me, can you say, 'Testing, one two'?"

"I can indeed, sir," says the derelict puzzledly. He clears his throat and says it quite well, although his pronunciation leaves something to be desired and his voice is a bit phlegmy from his life of degradation.

"Good enough," says Roy. "You are now a roadie. Report to my tour manager, who will check you for vermin and give you soup and an advance of money."

The degraded figure is overwhelmed with gratitude and touches his forelock several times, and I repress a tear of emotion at my friend's kindness. We give him the villains' bomb and knife to take to Roy's tour manager with instructions for them to be kept safely on a high shelf away from children.

The villain is snoring and unconscious. We check he is not badly injured, take the mysterious briefcase from his inert hand and leave the bad neighborhood with all possible haste.

Chapter 44

Roy and I flee through several streets until we are in a much nicer part of town and at last sit down breathlessly at a table at an open-air cafe in a crowded square. Here surely we will be safe from everything save the occasional trick-cyclist or yo-yo show-off.

"We must find a policeman," I say, "and report our ill-usage and give them the briefcase."

"Hold," says Roy, "a problem arises. The briefcase is not ours and for all we can prove belongs to those scoundrels. As far as legal nicety goes we are in the wrong in depriving them of it."

"It is so," I admit glumly.

"Besides . . . ," says Roy darkly, "I do not wish to cast aspersions, but can we trust the police to return the case to its rightful owners? We do not know how far the conspiracy has spread. Think how easily those villains infiltrated the press."

I am appalled. "You mean . . . ?"

"I mean we should trust no one but ourselves. This thing may go all the way to the top. Even the Düsseldorf town council may be implicated."

I slump in my chair with horror. But I am then forced to correct my slovenly posture when a waiter appears to take our order.

"What can make this case so valuable to the ruffians?" says Roy when he has departed.

"We can only surmise, Roy. Perhaps it contains jewels or bullion or index-linked bonds or sacred relics or the plans for an efficient new weapon." I examine the case hesitantly. "Perhaps if we were to take a look inside? It is irregular to the point of outrage but it may provide some answers."

"I believe it would be justified," says Roy. "We have higher motives than vulgar curiosity."

I say, "Logically as you are a performer I should be the one to open it in case it is booby-trapped and blows my face off."

"That is kind of you."

I hand Jetta across the table and say, "If I should be killed I entreat you to raise her as if she were your own."

"I will do so."

I take a deep breath and lift the lid. Fortunately there is no booby trap but what I see renders me stunned and speechless.

"It is beautiful," I manage to gasp.

"Come," says Roy impatiently after a few moments. "Do not leave me groping in the dark without a candle. What is it? What fantastic prize can have driven men to steal, cheat, lie, manhandle, kidnap and attempt murder by earwigs? Is it bullion? Diamonds? Jewelry? Banknotes? Rare spices or unguents from the exotic Orient? Scientific formulas? Military secrets?"

"It is something more precious than any of them . . ." I breathe.

"So?" says Roy curiously.

And I take out from the briefcase a silvery rod.

"It is clingfilm!"

To be resumed!

But now the demands of my carefully crafted plot require that I transport you back to the villains.

The chief villain quickly comes to and looks up and down the street for us, but we have gone. Saying "Bah" and stamping his foot, he logically proceeds upstairs to where the other villains and his mother are tied up.

"Oh, boss," says the third villain in relief, "are we glad to see you! You will never guess what has happened."

But soon they are not so glad to see him, for after untying them and checking they are not hurt he proceeds to swear, rebuke, snarl and stamp his foot at them for letting us get away until they are cringing and downcast. He is so angry that they want to go to the toilet but are scared to ask permission.

"It would appear," he hisses in conclusion, "that you imbibed inefficiency with your mother's milk and cut your teeth upon a diet of raw ineptitude!"

The other two villains look sad and forlorn.

"As for you, Mother," he says to the old woman, "I am ashamed at your lack of diligence. If Father was here he would doubtless rap you over the knuckles with a ninja flail and throw you in the dustbin, like in the good old days."

"That he would not," cries the old crone defiantly, "for the dustbin is too full to fit me in, for I never empty it!"

"Ah, Mutti!" says Heinrich with a grudging twinge of affection, and smashes a chair over her head.

Lothar bashfully raises his hand.

"May I go to the toilet?" he asks in a small voice.

"You may not!" yells the chief villain. "As punishment for your inefficiency you must hold it in until I say so."

"But he could do himself a mischief that way," points out Otto.

"Shut up!" snarls Heinrich. "He may burst his bladder or even produce a damp stain for all I care!"

He paces up and down with a face like thunder.

"There is only one thing for it," he growls at last. "I am forced to contact our dark spymasters for further instructions!"

The other two villains wring their hands and bite their nails at this, for their dark spymasters are even more scary than he is. Even Heinrich is reluctant.

"Must we do so?" ventures Otto at last. "Could we not attempt to resolve the situation ourselves, and only mention it to our dark spymasters many years from now in a confessional moment over schnapps?"

"Or send them a postcard full of general chit-chat," suggests Lothar, "and mention the loss of the briefcase in a casual and light-hearted PS? That is often the best way to break bad news."

Heinrich is tempted by this for a moment but finally shakes his head. "No, no, we must make contact now. Have you a phone, Mother?"

"That I have," says his mother somewhat shakily, still picking splinters of chair out of her head, "but it does not work, for I never pay the bill!"

"Ordinarily your compulsive iniquity would amuse me, Mother, but not now." Bad-temperedly Heinrich breaks another chair over his mother's head and stamps downstairs to find a phone booth.

He dials a certain number which does not go through the ordinary phone exchanges but rather through a secret criminal phone system in which the operators are all sworn to secrecy and are deaf mutes anyway. Well, not deaf, but they are all villainesses and recruited from the ranks of retired floozies and injured ninjas and so forth.

The phone is answered by a man known only as Der Skorpion, which may be loosely translated as "The Scorpion." He is twenty times as scary as Heinrich. If I was forced to describe him to you, you would very likely faint, but fortunately I do not have to do so.

He has a finger in every pie, in the rather unhygienic expression. He controls evil bandits in Mexico, vicious samurai in Japan, fiendish tax avoidance schemes in the Bahamas and lewd milkmaids in Bavaria.

"Good day," he says to Heinrich, "are you well?"

"I am very well, thank you," says Heinrich. "And you?"

"Oh, a little heartburn and indigestion after meals, but I cannot complain," says the criminal mastermind. "Or at least, if I did, no one would care, for everyone around me is evil." He suddenly feels sad. Even a criminal mastermind can get lonely. Briskly he returns the call to business. "Well, why have you rung the secret emergency number?" he asks.

"Oh, you know, I just wanted to make small talk," lies Heinrich, suddenly nervous and remembering Lothar's idea of blending bad news in with general chit-chat. "For example, how is your golf nowadays?"

"Not very good since I got a giant metal claw instead of an arm," admits the number one villain sadly. I told you he was scary. "On the plus side, of course, whenever anyone beats me at golf I am able to snip their limbs off with it."

"Ha ha ha," laughs Heinrich falsely. "Lovely story. Well, be seeing you."

"Oh, Heinrich," says his boss smoothly, "while I have you, may I inquire how our business is progressing with that extremely valuable briefcase?"

"I am sorry, I did not hear that, the line is a bad one," lies Heinrich quickly.

"The line is in order and he asked about the briefcase," says the criminal phone operator sharply.

Heinrich's palms sweat. "I have to report that we have lost the briefcase." Quickly he recounts the errors of the past two days.

"Oh well, never mind," says his boss. "I am sure that you tried your best and you know I am too big a man to hold it against you or ever seek to take some horrible revenge."

Heinrich is pleasantly relieved for a moment and then realizes he is being sarcastic. His boss's sinister voice is so subtle and silky in its implication of menace that often people think he is actually being friendly and only become scared hours later just when they are happily reading a book or enjoying a nice hot bath, which is then spoiled.

"You know how much money this was worth to us," his superior continues. "We have a lot of overheads maintaining our vast criminal network and now we may have to issue a profit warning for this quarter to our dark shareholders. You are . . . a disappointment to me."

Heinrich gulps, for to be a disappointment to Der Skorpion does not mean ordinary things such as you and I might expect when we have disappointed someone, such as being written out of a will or being expelled from catering college or your parents moving away to a new location and not telling you their address or being banned from dating agencies and marriage bureaus or being divorced on the grounds of extreme and improbable mental cruelty—it means being sewn into a mailbag full of earwigs and dropped into a pond.

"No man can plan for the random malice of fate," he protests feebly.

"On the contrary," says his boss, "I have planned for every contingency, including this one. Your biggest error was not contacting me immediately the first time the briefcase was taken. For prudent precautions were taken before it was passed on to you and it will be very simple to find it again."

Heinrich's eyes widen as his boss informs him of something. But I will not tell you what it is just yet for the sake of heightened suspense.

"Also," says Heinrich, "no wonder they call you a criminal mastermind."

"I know, I am wonderful, arguably the most efficient criminal since records began," boasts his boss shamelessly. "But you will be called criminally negligent if you fail in this matter again! I will send reinforcements if you require them but you must succeed at all costs!"

"I will do so," Heinrich assures him zealously. He clears his throat. "I was wondering," he says casually, "what is actually inside the briefcase to make it so valuable to us?" He has been forbidden to look inside the briefcase, although he did lift the lid a tiny inch and take a quick peek before becoming scared, and also felt around inside it a bit, as that was not technically looking. However, all he perceived was some velvet lining and he thought perhaps they were carrying stolen carpet swatches. "Naturally I do not care myself but the other two were curious," he lies.

"That is not needful for you to know," says the Skorpion harshly. "Remember the penalty for undue curiosity!" Heinrich swallows, for the penalty for undue curiosity is something really foul that leaves you a broken and pitiful man who is unable to even tie his own shoelaces without help from a nurse. Not that Heinrich ever bothers to tie his shoelaces—but it is nice to know he could if he wanted to. "However, I will tell you this much: it is possibly the greatest thing this world has ever seen! Apart from me, of course," he adds boastfully.

His voice becomes an icy snarl.

"Recover the briefcase and make an example of this Orbison and his friends. When you find them you must kill them, ransack their houses, confiscate their possessions and put their terrapin to work on a farm!"

Meanwhile back in the town square Roy and I mull over our discovery.

"This makes no sense," says Roy. "Who on earth could be so possessive about clingfilm?"

I study my nails and pointedly say nothing. He can be a very stupid and thoughtless man at times.

Still it is somewhat baffling. I myself would go to extreme lengths to obtain a roll of clingfilm at need, but even I have not gone much further than to wake a supermarket manager in the middle of the night or hire a van and journey to Köln or Aachen when there has not been enough in the local stores to satisfy my demands.

And I would even say that it is possible to become attached to a particular roll of clingfilm, for after intense and cultivated study one can perceive that each individual roll has its own particular quirks and idiosyncrasies. One will unroll with a sticky rasp, one with an eager *schlurrp*, another with a teasing *mrrp* or still another with a splendid sound like *fhooop*. One will be wrinkled, one flawlessly smooth, one wrinkled in places but smooth in other places, and so forth. A sentimental man might even have his special favorites and give them nicknames and even in whimsical moments affect to hold conversations with them. I imagine.

Yet there is undoubtedly some mystery here, for the villains struck me as coarse and unrefined types and not at all likely to be clingfilm connoisseurs. The chief baddy was eager enough to steal mine, and yet he evinced no particular joy in possessing it and planned to sell it to a tinker.

What then can be so special about this particular roll to make them cheat, steal, and menace with earwigs to obtain it? I examine the roll minutely and can perceive nothing unusual. Yet it was mounted smoothly in a fitted groove in the case as though the case had been designed specially to carry it. I make a mental note that this is a very good idea and one I should perhaps emulate, and even refine—after all, there would have been room for more than one roll in a briefcase, and one could perhaps fit a false bottom for purposes of concealment in situations where one feared confiscation.

"Perhaps," I theorize, "this roll has some historical significance, and is more in the realm of an artifact than merely a household necessity or luxury toy. Perhaps it once wrapped the picnic sandwiches or party leftovers of some crowned head of Europe. Perhaps"—and my eyes light up—"perhaps it is the first roll of clingfilm ever manufactured, in which case it would be semi-legendary and almost divine—why, a man might dare anything to obtain such a prize!"

"It is a mistake to theorize without all the facts." Roy is examining the case minutely. "Hold," he suddenly says, "perceive here—there is writing on the exterior of the case." It is so—in discreet embossed letters we had not noticed before are the words *Top Secret*.

"Also. . ." I say. "What can that portend?"

"And what is this?" he exclaims. He has removed the fitted velvet lining that held the roll. Revealed beneath it is a small metal gadget that has a radio aerial and a flashing light.

"Why," I say, "as it happens I know what that is. It is a radio location transmitter. It beams a signal that reveals its whereabouts to whoever has the appropriate tracking device. It was featured on *Guten Abend Düsseldorf*'s 'Brave New World with Lorna Bratkartoffeln' segment. I considered fitting one to Jetta's collar in case she was ever carried off by gypsies."

"Whoever could have fitted such futuristic technology to a briefcase?"

"Why," I say, "either the original owners of the briefcase, or—"

"Or?" Prompts Roy. "It is a mistake to leave sentences unfinished."

But for a moment I am unable to speak and can only stare rudely over Roy's shoulder.

"Or someone else who is very attached to the briefcase!" I eventually conclude. "Look, Roy!"

Roy looks. "*Ach*," he says, "this is an untoward development."

The three villains have entered the square! They are frowning at a small gadget with a long antenna, which they are waving around.

What has happened is that following their dark spymaster's instructions they have locked onto the briefcase with a radio tracker and come rushing to the square to apprehend us, with only a brief toilet stop for Lothar.

"Quick, Roy! They are tracking the case."

Quickly Roy smashes the radio beacon.

I see the chief villain scowl and shake his gadget, then check his batteries and finally throw it on the ground and stamp on it petulantly.

"Good work. They can no longer trace us. But they know we are in the square somewhere!"

As they turn to scan the crowd we hold our hands in front of our faces so they cannot see us and I drape a napkin over Jetta. But such poor camouflage cannot hold at close range.

We watch as the chief villain takes out his gun and mutters instructions to his confederates, who space out around the edge of the plaza to cover the exits. For Roy and me there can surely be no escape . . .

Now what can transpire? You must wait on tenterhooks to find out!

Chapter 45

Cunningly the three villains have spaced themselves out around the edges of the square and are working their way in. They are rudely staring at people's faces at close range to make sure they are not us in disguise, checking under tables, and even poking and shaking people's poodles and so forth to make sure they are not really terrapins.

This will make a great scene for a film, for it is very menacing.

"Our disguise will not hold," says Roy. "There can be only seconds before we are brutally shot down with bullets."

"It is so," I say.

"Come, my friend, use your ingenuity. I have faith you will contrive some ingenious scheme to avert disaster."

Desperately I look around.

"There is one thing we might try!" I cry. "Behold, the fountain!" I point to the fountain that is in the center of the square.

"I am beholding the fountain," says Roy. "State the thought that has entered your brain."

"It is forbidden to frolic in the fountain, but I am sure the city fathers did not envisage the possibility of citizens being chased and killed when they drew up that bylaw. If we were to climb into the fountain and hold our breaths and lie down at the bottom of the pool, we may thereby evade detection until the villains have passed by."

"The way is plain," says Roy. "We will climb into the fountain and lie down underwater at once."

"But hold," I say thoughtfully. "It strikes me that if we do so we will become wet."

"It is so," admits Roy.

"For myself it does not matter so much, for I have many clothes that I can wear. But for you as a style icon. . .if anyone beheld you in a sodden state you must henceforth be known as the man in trademark wet clothing. Moreover you are holding the briefcase, which is made of costly leather and may be damaged by the water and is not our property to be cavalier with."

"You speak the truth," says Roy. "At all costs I must avoid becoming wet. Yet it is hard to embrace a brutal death by fired bullets as the alternative."

"Wait, though!" A ray of dawn breaks. "I have the clingfilm from the briefcase. Although it is not our property there can be no harm in borrowing some in this dire extremity. How would it be if I was to completely wrap you in it? You would thereby be enabled to enter the waters of the fountain without becoming wet."

"How simple you make things," says Roy. He rises. "Commence to wrap me in clingfilm at once."

I start from the ankles and work my way up. I must work quickly, lest we be shot to death, and yet thoroughly and watertightly. But if I could not linger a few moments to enjoy it there would be no point being alive anyway. It is strange to be wrapping him in public in broad daylight but somehow thrilling in an illicit way. Soon, Roy Orbison is completely wrapped in clingfilm. I am a limp trembling leaf blown on a wind of exaltation.

"You are completely wrapped in clingfilm," I say. "Now if you will hop into the fountain—"

But it is too late! For the villains are upon us.

"Aha!" says the spy in the bandit hat, pointing his gun. "Now I have caught you! Give me that briefcase back at once or it will go badly with you!"

"We will not do so!" I say.

"Then pay the price!" And he points the gun at me and pulls the trigger!

I am filled with horror and say my prayers—but to my worse horror my life is spared, for Roy bravely comes hopping between us to take the bullet for me!

The gun is fired and the bullet speeds into Roy. . .

Reader, I had logically intended to end upon this cliff-hanger but I find I am not cruel enough and must tell you immediately what happens next.

For the happy and amazing truth is that Roy is not harmed—indeed, the bullet appears to simply bounce off him! It speeds back toward the villains and grazes the ear of Lothar, who says "Ow!" in a hurt and resentful tone, before shooting a chip of stone out of the fountain, which, alas, will have to be repaired.

Heinrich scowls and curses and shoots Roy several more times at point-blank range, but each time the bullets simply bounce off! They go ricocheting across the square, but fortunately no passersby are hurt apart from a trick-cyclist who is shot in the knee and lamed for life and will have to find some less dangerous profession.

Otto and Lothar cross themselves and mutter "Unglaublich."

I more rationally can perceive that the bullets are bouncing off Roy's clingfilm wrapping! Yet how can that be? Clingfilm has many virtues, yet I had not suspected this one. A wrapping of many many many layers might perhaps slow down a bullet, but surely not a simple waterproofing wrap such as I have just administered. Something unusual is at work here.

"So," says Heinrich, frowning, "for reasons I cannot fathom it would appear that thanks to your wrapping of clingfilm you are immune to my bullets. Or . . . are you?" He cackles evilly and lowers his gun . . . to point at Roy's shoes! "I could still shoot your feet and give you a slow death by bleeding and embarrassment at the damaged state of your shoewear." Roy flinches somewhat. "Or," continues the villain, "I could simply do this!" And he reaches out and barbarously tears a great hole in the clingfilm around Roy's chest! Truly he is a man who holds nothing sacred.

"Now," he says, pointing his gun at Roy's unwrapped chest, "prepare to be shot in the heart or lungs!"

And here, reader, I am afraid I must insist upon calling a cliff-hanger—and no peeking at the next chapter until you have put in some hand-wringing time!

Chapter 46

Fortunately before the villain can shoot Roy in the torso a policeman comes.

"What is going on here?" he asks sternly.

The villain attempts to hide his gun and looks nonchalant.

"Nothing," he lies smoothly. "We are playing a game, a nice game. We are playing at running races and this is the starting pistol."

"There is no running in the public squares," says the policeman forbiddingly. "Who is the ringleader here?"

The two junior villains instinctively look at the chief villain and are about to say, "He is," but quickly he stamps on their feet so that instead they hop and say "Ouch" and "What was that for?" in hurt voices.

The chief villain points at Roy and says, "He is! And the other man and his terrapin. See how suspiciously he is dressed, wrapped in some strange futuristic substance!"

"It is so," says the policeman, stroking his moustache thoughtfully. "Do you have a license to be wrapped up like that in public?"

My palms sweat. The policeman is sure to confiscate our clingfilm and then obtain a search warrant for my house and confiscate the rest of my clingfilm and then send me to jail for clingfilm-hoarding and send Jetta to a home for delinquent animals.

Roy makes muffled noises which serve only to exasperate the policeman. Quickly I say, "Dear policeman, indeed he has a license—artistic license! For this is none other than Roy Orbison, the well-known rock minstrel and man in black, and he surely cannot be held to the same standards as other people."

"I am afraid I have not heard of this Roy Orbison!" says the policeman.

"Oh, Mr. Policeman, surely you have heard of Roy Orbison," says the chief villain surprisingly. He leans close to the policeman's ear and lies smoothly, "Why, he is the rock singer who releases wild and seditious songs with titles such as 'Down with Policemen' and 'Undermine the EU' and 'Let's Go Crazy Wild and Ride on Trams without Paying' and 'Give Me VAT Reform or Give Me Death.' They are all on his album *I Licked the Knees of the Devil's Daughter*. And played at his concert 'An Evening of Raucous Impoliteness with Roy Orbison.'"

He nudges the other villains. "It is so," they mutter, shifty-eyed, blushing somewhat at the barefaced lie which shocks even them.

The policeman's cheeks turn a beetroot color as he becomes angry.

"It is not so!" I cry in outrage. Roy makes noises of protest while Jetta seems to shake her head, although maybe she is just bored and looking for worms. But the damage has been done.

"So, Mister Nihilistic Rock Dandy," says the policeman in tones of silky menace, "you think it is fun to connive at the overthrow of the state and lick people's knees, do you? Perhaps we should take you downtown and put you in a drafty cell with no supper while I obtain a search warrant for your house—all your houses!" I almost faint. "And your terrapin will most likely be sent to a home for delinquent animals!"

The villain frowns somewhat at this. "Yes, you should do so," he says. "But first perhaps you will force these villains to return our property to us. For the reason we were chasing them is, they have stolen that briefcase which belongs to me!"

"This is not his briefcase!" I cry.

"Also," says the policeman, "then it is yours?"

"It is not mine," I say, sweating, "but—"

"See, he admits it! But I can prove it is mine," says the villain smoothly, "for my name is written on it."

The policeman peers closely at the briefcase beneath Roy's wrapping.

"The only writing I can see is the words *Top Secret*," he says puzzledly. "That is your name?"

"Indeed it is," says the villain grandly. "It is short for 'Topol Secret.'"

"You are Jewish?" says one of his henchmen in surprise.

"Hist," says Heinrich quietly, "I am fibbing."

But he has gone too far and by now the policeman is confused.

"I am confused," says the policeman, "for did you not at first say you were playing some nice if dangerous running game?"

"The truth wears many faces," says the villain unctuously.

"It is so," says the policeman thoughtfully, "but I think perhaps until this is all sorted out you had better come downtown too."

"On the contrary," says the villain with icy eloquence, "the only person who is going somewhere is you—to the land of unconsciousness . . . "

And the three villains jump on the policeman!

He struggles and orders them to stop but they do not obey him and soon he is unconscious and snoring on the ground, fettered with his own handcuffs and gagged with their unclean handkerchiefs.

Some passersby look alarmed and outraged, but the villains reassure them falsely that they are just playing a nice game.

"Now," says the chief villain Heinrich evilly, taking out his gun once more, "those other interfering fools will be put to death!"

But only I as a novelist know this, for while they were tussling with the policeman Roy and Jetta and I in the story took the opportunity to run away! Or in Roy's case hop away, for he is still wrapped in the clingfilm, although not completely.

"*Ach*, they have gone!" cry the villains in dismay.

"They are going into the park!" says Otto pointing. "They will get away!"

"No," says Heinrich. "They will not get away . . ."

"Surely we will be safe in the park!" I gasp as we run and hop for our lives. In our desperation we even run on the grass sometimes and through bushes, heedless of damage to our clothes and postponing the inevitable guilt.

But it appears I have spoken too soon. For suddenly in the middle of the park we are confronted with perhaps the most terrifying spectacle I have ever seen.

For from behind a wall there pops up—a whole army of Mexican bandits!

There are perhaps so many as thirty of them, all with sombreros and bandoliers and long scary moustaches, all of them firing their guns toward us!

Mexican bandits! In Düsseldorf! Is this the end of everything, as I have long feared it?

Surely this is a cliff-hanger to make a brave man scream! Cower in your homes until the next installment . . .

Chapter 47

We scream and flee from the Mexican bandits!

But little do we suspect that we have made an error . . .

For as we run and hop out of the park, from behind a wall in the opposite direction from the Mexican bandits seven cowboys appear with guns—one of whom has a familiar bald head . . .

Then a man in jodhpurs beats a riding crop against his leg and yells, "Cut!" And the Mexican bandits take off their sombreros and false moustaches and commence to talk amongst themselves quite urbanely and without stabbing each other—for they are merely actors and this is the set of Yul Brynner's new Magnificent Seven movie!

"Well," says Yul to the director, "how was the shot, Maestro?"

"While there was plenty of sunshine and no hairs in the gate, I regret to announce the shot was ruined, for a man carrying a terrapin and a man in black wrapped in clingfilm variously ran and hopped through the middle of it at the most dramatic moment!"

"Clingfilm?" Yul Brynner exchanges a significant glance with Jim Morrison, who has been hired to play a cameo as an Indian shaman. "So . . ."

"Surely that was Roy Orbison and his friend and terrapin!" says the *Rolling Stone* reporter, who was recovered from his ill-usage by the villains, although he continues to nurse a grudge against the *Düsseldorf Zeitung* and has canceled his subscription.

"Groovy," opines Morrison. "Those three cats sure do have fun!"

Little does he know we are not having fun at all but are being chased and killed.

"When you have finished talking please resume your places," says the director. "It is wasteful of celluloid but we must film the shot again, for a hopping man in clingfilm does not accord with my artistic vision."

Each to their own, I suppose. He is probably not a very good director.

"Hold," says the *Rolling Stone* reporter, who has been permitted to visit the film set provided he keeps a respectful distance and does not ask questions during filming, "that footage need not be wasted. If you are going to throw it out may I have it? I have a reason for asking."

"You need not specify that reason. You may take it and cut it into guitar picks for all I care," says the director grandly, somewhat contemptuous of this unmanly scavenging.

"You may only have a few more minutes of fine weather, Yul," admonishes Mitzi Klavierstuhl, who has been retained as weather consultant. "If you do not nail this shot before the next big cumulonimbus comes over I will not be answerable for the consequences."

"Then let us get back to work."

However, just then a further distraction appears in the shape of the three villains, who burst out of the bushes from the same direction we did, their leader waving his gun! When he sees the film crew the leader hastily puts his gun away and the other two study their nails and look nonchalant.

"Excuse me," says the chief spy to Yul, "did you happen to see a party consisting of Roy Orbison and friend and terrapin pass this way fleeing for their lives? I have a reason for asking."

"As it happens, we did," says Yul, "but I must ask you to state that reason."

"Oh—I am an old friend of his from North America," lies the wicked man easily. "We went to school together, you know. We met in the street just now but I find I neglected to give him my address."

"Also," says Yul. Something about the situation strikes him as odd and he decides to be careful. "And in which part of North America did you go to school with Roy?"

"Oh—I can never remember the name," says the deceiver. "It was somewhere near Greenland, I think." He has a theory that speed and confidence are more important in passing a lie than taking a suspicious amount of time to think up details.

Yul Brynner is not quite satisfied and suspiciously narrows his eyes.

However, the director impatiently says, "We do not have time for this! They went that way," and points.

The three villains bow their thanks, take out their gun, and with a cry of "After them!" rush off on our trail.

Yul Brynner thoughtfully rubs his bald head. "Something is amiss here," he says.

"I got a dark aura off that cat," says Jim Morrison in his mystical way. "I believe he was up to some mischief."

"Why cannot you make us bandit sombreros as authentic as that?" Yul overhears an extra complaining to the costume designer. "It even had a Mexican label and genuine bloodstains!"

"Also!" says Yul, clapping his cowboy hat on his trademark bald head. "Our friends may be in danger! I believe it is time for the Magnificent Seven to ride again! Let us chase those men and detain them!"

Outside the park Roy and I jump breathlessly into a convenient taxi.

"Drive around at random," I say to the driver, "although not so randomly that you drive off a bridge or we end up in Belgium."

"I understand what you mean," says the driver and we move off.

Roy makes muffled noises that may be "You may unwrap me now." On the other hand, I reflect, they may equally well be "At least the weather is fine" or "I hope the driver does not gyp us" or "I do not wish to go to Belgium" or for that matter "I hope you do not unwrap me," so I do not unwrap him. However, he keeps repeating those noises and wriggling about, so eventually I sternly force my rebelling hand to unwrap him.

"It is my worst fear come true," I say. "Düsseldorf has been overrun by Mexican bandits! We must alert the authorities at once!"

"Which authorities can we trust?" says Roy, who has been turned regrettably cynical by the events of the day. "See how easily they suborned the policeman. To say nothing of the park-keepers, who must be turning a blind eye to Mexican bandits walking on the grass. Let us face the bitter fact that the conspiracy reaches into all walks of life and Düsseldorf is a whited sepulchre. The only person I would trust with this is my good friend Queen Elizabeth, and alas I have forgotten her phone number."

"I am certainly not keen on tangling with the police again," I admit. "Jetta could not cope with a home for delinquent animals."

"We are thrown back on our own resources," says Roy. "Let us examine this confounded briefcase again in hope of unraveling this tangled skein."

Frowning, he scrutinizes every inch of the briefcase minutely, even going so far as to peer over his dark glasses at one point for keener vision. He holds it upside down and shakes it about but we are none the wiser. But then—

"Hold!" he cries. "What is this?"

He has again removed the velvet-lined tray designed to hold the clingfilm and then prized out the villains' broken radio-tracker under it. Revealed beneath, pasted neatly onto the underside of the case, is a card which reads: "Attention! If lost or stolen please return this briefcase to the following address! A reward and many thanks will be offered."

And below is printed the address of the briefcase's original owners!

"Now dawn breaks!" cries Roy joyfully. "We can return the item to the rightful property holder."

"You know," I say thoughtfully, "it strikes me that that address is a familiar one . . ."

Roy takes out the card and passes it to the driver.

"Desist your random meanderings and make the car go to that address with all legal haste," he instructs.

"I will do so."

"Now to reach the bottom of this mystery," says Roy.

He puts the case back together and, somewhat reluctantly, I put the mysterious roll of clingfilm back into it.

Presently we find ourselves in the industrial side of town.

"You have arrived at your destination," the driver informs us, pulling up outside a gate and putting on the handbrake. "Please pay me now."

"We will do so," I say. "Thank you for a smooth journey."

We pay him and get out.

Through the gate we are confronted with a large and splendid factory.

Roy frowns. "Unless the driver is a part of the conspiracy or has taken us to the wrong destination for reasons of inefficiency or random malice, we will find the answers we seek here. I confess I had expected the house or laboratory of some white-haired rocket scientist or the imposing marble halls of some lofty government department rather than a humble manufactory."

"Roy—" I say.

But just then a whistle blows. Lines of workers commence to file out of the doors of the factory and out of the gate, commending each other on the day's labor satisfactorily completed and good-naturedly chaffing each other on the prospects for the various sports teams they follow by way of letting down their hair.

"We should not be seen," says Roy, holding a hand before his face so that his trademark dark glasses will not be recognized and ducking down an alley. "There is no telling how far the conspiracy has spread."

"But Roy—" I say.

There is something I urgently wish to tell him but I cannot find words to do so.

Some way down the alley Roy locates a side door. "It is irregular, but we will enter this way," he says. Reluctantly I follow. He opens the door and says, "The place seems deserted now. Let us proceed."

"But Roy," I say, but Roy has already proceeded inside. I look to Jetta for advice but she merely looks at me unblinkingly. I hesitate for a moment. "What can I do?" I tell her. "There seems no option in this case." Jetta looks studiedly neutral and retracts her head some way back into her shell, although perhaps she is only cold.

So I follow Roy through the door.

We find ourselves in the main workshop, a vast and magnificent edifice filled with splendid shiny machinery. Though the machines are quiet and inactive now, they still retain an epic grandeur. So hygienic and well-kept is it that if one had not seen the hale and hearty workers one might surmise the place was staffed by some benevolent pixies or elf-folk. Especially when one beholds, stretching in merry ribbons and gay streamers from one gleaming machine to the next, crisscrossing the room, spilling from apertures, spooled around bobbins, or wound about tubes and stacked neatly in countless wonderful piles reaching almost to the heavens, a certain ethereal, twinkling, hypnotic, miraculously translucent substance . . .

"What manner of place is this?" says Roy.

I repress the urge to yodel.

"I am back in the clingfilm factory!" I cry.

To be continued as soon as possible!

Chapter 48

"I am back in the clingfilm factory," I repeat.

All around me the mighty machines are towering and gleaming like some funfair of joy. Everywhere there is clingfilm in profound abundance, everywhere the means for making more, wellsprings of happiness that can never dry up. This is God's own playground.

"I am back in the clingfilm factory," I say again.

The cathedral of untrammeled delight stretches around me in every direction. Everywhere the eye alights is some fresh sight to fill the heart with helium. Acre upon lovely acre of clingfilm piled upon clingfilm, trolleys and conveyor belts full of clingfilm, bolts and bundles and boxes of it, crates and carts and carousels packed tight with glinting batons of pellucid wonder, clingfilm sufficient to wrap a small nation of black-clad pop troubadours, if such a happy nation existed, and if they gave permission.

How many generations of mankind did it take to reach this summit? Was this dream always in our hearts from the time we crawled out of the first primeval swamp? Has it always been before us, a guiding light for the visionaries and idealists to grope toward? Who can tell. It has taken much sacrifice to reach this shining city, but none can behold it and not feel exalted.

"There is no time to be lost," says Roy. "Let us locate someone in authority and get to the bottom of this mystery. Which way do you suggest we go?"

"I am back in the clingfilm factory," I say one more time. "For legal reasons I prefer not to disclose, I am not supposed to come within five hundred yards of this building."

"There can be no objection in the present circumstances," says Roy.

"I am back in the clingfilm factory," I agree.

Just then a door opens and a man in a white coat appears.

He stops dead when he sees me and his mouth hangs open in alarm.

"Oh God," he says. "It is you."

"I am back in the clingfilm factory," I explain. "I am very sorry for the intrusion but this time I have an excellent reason no lawyer or doctor could possibly find fault with."

"Please do not kiss my hands or feet," says the man, who is the manager of the factory and whom I have met before. "And do not start singing hymns."

"No, no," I say, "I will not do so. I am over that now. I understand now that you are not the man who invented clingfilm but merely a very fortunate man who is privileged to serve as high priest of this temple."

"Oh God," he says. "It is starting again."

"Forgive me," I say. "I will not speak in this way for I know it alarms you. I understand that the demands of efficiency and modesty require that you affect an air of nonchalance and treat this as any other job. I will keep my admiration within bounds."

"Please do not yodel," says the man. "And do not recite your clingfilm mantras. They disturb me."

"I will not do so."

"Do not roll your eyes or nuzzle the machinery. And do not do . . . those other things you would do."

"I am back in the clingfilm factory!"

"Oh God."

"I do not like to interrupt," says Roy, "but we have more pressing matters to deal with."

"Speak softly, Roy," I say in hushed and reverent tones, "we are in the presence of an awe-inspiring amount of clingfilm."

"That's it, I am calling the police," says the manager.

"You should do so," says Roy. "That is, if you are sure you can trust them with this."

He holds forth the briefcase and opens it to reveal the half-used roll of clingfilm.

"The stolen prototype!" cries the manager. "You have found it!"

"We have gone to a lot of trouble for that briefcase and risked life and limb to bring it to you," says Roy.

"Then you have saved the free world from destruction and this company from bankruptcy!" says the manager. "I must thank you. Both of you," he adds, with a somewhat grudging bow to me.

"I am back in the clingfilm factory," I say amiably. "With Roy . . ."

"I do not wish to pry, but would you explain what all this is about?" says Roy.

"By all means," says the manager. "This is a secret prototype of an experimental super-clingfilm we have designed for the military. It is designed to be bulletproof for use in war zones. I am sure I do not have to explain the tactical advantages of troops being able to take their own packed lunches into battle with them and keep them fresh for many days."

"I am no military historian," says Roy, "but even I can think of many conflicts whose outcome may have been different had there been a supply of fresh salad at hand."

"Unfortunately the prototype was stolen by a shadowy cabal of miscreants we believe intended to sell it to the highest bidder. We had despaired of ever getting it back. You will both be rewarded as you deserve!"

"It was not all our work," says Roy modestly. "This plucky little terrapin, Jetta, deserves much of the credit."

"Then she shall be rewarded too!"

"They will all be rewarded," suddenly says a voice of silken menace from behind us, "but not as they expect. . ."

And we turn and see the three villains!

We gulp nervously. The lead villain still has his gun. One of the other two has picked up a plank with many dangerous splinters in it and the other is holding his hand in such a way as to suggest he is either prepared to use karate on us or administer a resounding slap on the cheek.

"Yes," hisses the chief villain in tones of icy ill-will, "we have followed you! Now we will kill you and take back the briefcase, and afterwards ransack your houses and confiscate all your belongings!"

"You will not do so," says Roy. He closes the briefcase and we run! The manager shrieks and goes to call the police but is shot in the foot and ends up hopping and saying "Ouch."

The villains pursue us through the deserted factory, firing their gun. Bullets go whizzing past our heads. One hits a button that starts the machinery and as the glorious contraptions whirr into life I take a moment to marvel at the wondrous mechanical whirligigs endlessly producing softly glinting ribbons of clingfilm, cascading and shimmering like rivers in the Garden of Eden. Streamers of clingfilm crisscross the room from spindle to spindle. All about us clingfilm is disgorged, spooled, bobbined, measured and packed. In spite of our peril I watch mesmerized as virginal young cardboard tubes queue eagerly to be wound up with clingfilm, as they are duly consecrated and dropped into their boxes, as the individual boxes are packed into bulk delivery cartons, and as the cartons are slid onto a conveyor belt and each consignment is trundled through a machine where they themselves are wrapped with even more clingfilm before being dispatched to avid customers all over the world. I stifle a tear of awe as we flee.

We run up steps to a high metal walkway with the villains hot on our heels.

"You will not get away!" says the lead villain, firing bullets at us.

"On the contrary, we will," says Roy defiantly, but it is more bravado than anything else, for now there is no place else to run!

For at the other end of the walkway we see one of the other villains has efficiently run to cut us off and is brandishing his splintery plank menacingly.

"*Ach*," says Roy, "now we are liable to be killed. Fate is a jesting harlot. I never thought to die in a clingfilm factory."

As for me I have thought of it several times, although I thought it would be from bliss rather than an assassin's bullet.

Cackling, the villains close in on us, variously waving their gun, their plank, and their hand. We stand back to back and prepare to meet our fate with defiance.

"It is all up with us, old friend," says Roy. "For my part I could ask for no finer companions in doom than yourself and Jetta."

"Likewise, Roy," I say. Jetta for her part merely looks stoical.

I reflect that there are indeed worse fates than to die here and in such company and in the cause of defending clingfilm. Wryly I muse that if heaven awaits it cannot be very different from this wonderful place. I take a last regretful look at the whirling bobbins and humming machines and busy conveyor belts spread out majestically below us . . .

But hold! The way is plain!

"There is one thing we might try," I say excitedly. "Excuse me, Roy, I am afraid I must manhandle you now, but it is for your own good."

"Do what seems needful," says Roy. "I give you carte blanche in this extremity."

I bow and push Roy off the walkway and jump down after him. We land on a conveyor belt spread with cartons and boxes—heading toward the inviting mouth of a splendid construction labeled WRAPPING MACHINE! Above us on the walkway the villains snarl and gnash their teeth as we are conveyed quickly into the heart of the mechanism. As we lie there side by side benevolent metal arms raise us gently and tender robot hands clutching clingfilm whirl around us again and again, cocooning us snugly in it. Soon, myself and Jetta and Roy Orbison are completely wrapped in clingfilm together. I am consumed without trace in a conflagration of rapture.

"We are completely wrapped in clingfilm," I say, somewhat muffled.

Popped out of the other side of the wrapping machine, we slide down a chute and end up upright on an automated trolley, which whizzes us off across the factory and through a swing door.

Cursing, the villains descend from the gantry to give chase. But just then the front door bursts open and Yul Brynner and the Magnificent Seven rush in, firing their pistols in the air and waving lariats. Frightened, the villains run away.

But while I as the author know this, I in the story remain unaware of it for many weeks, for Roy and Jetta and I, completely wrapped in clingfilm together, are automatically trundled through a warehouse, tipped onto another conveyor belt, weighed, labeled, stamped, raised on an elevator, picked up by a crane, dropped down a chute, dumped onto a passing train and shipped to Vladivostok.

Chapter 49

The three villains flee through the streets.

"This is not over!" the leader snarls. "We will obtain reinforcements. Just let me get to a phone box and I will have a planeload of Mexican bandits here by tomorrow!"

Suddenly they pull up short, for they have come to a main street and the traffic light is against them. The two junior spies go to a designated crossing point and wait for the light to change, but the chief villain sneers at them.

"*Pah!*" he says. "What a pair of Boy Scouts! There is no time for that. I intend to take my chances and cross against the light!"

"You should not do so," the spy known as Otto cautions.

"Watch and you will see me do so!"

Quickly he looks both ways, sees his chance and dashes.

However, halfway across disaster strikes. For he trips over his shoelaces, which he never bothers to tie, and goes sprawling headlong in the middle of the road!

Cursing, he picks himself up. But to their horror the other two spies see a bus speeding toward him from behind.

"Look out, Heinrich!" cries Otto. "A bus is coming!"

But you will remember that Heinrich was not the chief spy's real name! Wedded to deception, he had meanly refused to divulge his real name and Heinrich was a fiction. Therefore he does not react to it now but merely frowns in confusion. By the time he realizes that he is meant to be Heinrich the bus is already upon him. Belatedly he attempts to jump out of the way, but his reflexes are slow due to his lack of sleep and he is run over and squashed.

An ambulance comes and rushes him to the hospital. He is a broken and mangled man but there is still a slim chance of saving his life. However, as he is not wearing clean underwear the surgeons hesitate to operate on him and he dies.

Moreover as his mother's stolen bra is later found in his pocket he is assumed to be a pervert and has to be buried in a special cemetery for cross-dressers, which causes much amusement in the criminal fraternity. His mother puts her head in the oven in shame, but there is no gas as she never pays the bill, and so the earwigs and cockroaches that infest it nibble her face off, because she never cleans it.

At the hospital his two cohorts hug each other and shed a tear or two for their fallen leader when they are informed of his demise, yet they cannot deny there is a certain justice in what has happened and that his criminal lifestyle brought about his downfall.

"I have learned my lesson," says Otto. "From now on I will eschew crime and take the straight and narrow path."

"I too."

"I shall devote my days to promoting safety in crossing the road."

"I for my part will realize my dream of opening a small florist. Those who have been victims of my crimes will receive a 7 percent discount or be given a free tulip upon proof of injury or mental stress."

Hand in hand they leave the hospital, mellowed and chastened.

"You know," says Otto thoughtfully, "there is one other good thing to come out of this."

"State that thing."

"We now have ammunition for a letter to Greta Sonderbar of 'Spooky Occurrences'! For earlier today did we not see a man shot several times and the bullets bounce off him?"

"Also..." breathes Lothar excitedly. "If we admit to being reformed criminals and say that is the miracle that reformed us, she may even have us on the show!"

"Quick! To the stationer's to steal some paper and a pen!"

"You mean—buy them!"

"Oh yes!" Laughing, they make off along the rocky road to redemption.

Little else remains to tell. The weeks pass pleasantly for Roy and Jetta and me, securely wrapped in clingfilm in the hold of the ship. There is a sufficiency of air trapped with us and we are able to lick the condensation formed by the moisture from our breaths.

All too soon we are unloaded at a warehouse in Vladivostok. When they behold us the workers utter obscure oaths originating from the Slavic steppes of their youth and call on Lenin's ghost to protect them. They scratch their heads as they puzzle over what to do with us. Eventually they put more labels and stamps on us and ship us back to Germany via the Pacific Ocean.

En route we are shipwrecked, however, and washed up on a deserted South Seas island. For some days we lie happily on the beach watching spectacular tropical sunsets and feeling the waves lapping gently against our clingfilm-wrapped feet.

Presently we are rescued and conveyed to Lima, still in our clingfilm wrapping. Due to a dock strike we are marooned there for some time, propped up in a corner of a shed with not much view and little to do besides playing I Spy in somewhat muffled voices. I find it congenial enough but Jetta grows impatient and attempts to chew her way out of the clingfilm, but eventually gives up and hibernates.

I will not weary you with details of our journeys across South America, on trains, on lorries, and lashed to the back of llamas. En route we are kidnapped by a tribe of jungle primitives who install us in a temple for a time and worship us as gods. Fortunately we escape the attentions of bandits.

At Buenos Aires we are loaded onto another ship. Due to a routing error we are sent back across the Pacific and visit Singapore and Hong Kong and half a dozen other places before eventually being dispatched to Europe via the Suez Canal.

In Egypt we are mistakenly placed on a canal barge and find ourselves for a time idling on a wharf along the Nile, our clingfilm coating thankfully protecting us from the harsh desert sun. We are within sight of a pyramid. Is it my imagination or does it seem familiar to me . . . ? Roy too seems a trifle preoccupied. Is there some significance here . . . who can tell?

We are carried in a camel train halfway across North Africa. At one point we are briefly drafted into the French Foreign Legion and used as a sandbag in an exciting battle with dervishes.

Eventually we are sent back in the right direction. We cross the Mediterranean without mishap and soon find ourselves being poled into Venice lying in a gondola. From there we are conveyed home by rail via Vienna, Köln and the Düsseldorf branch line before finally a homely delivery van drops us off back in the warehouse of the clingfilm factory. It chances to be a Friday, however, and we are not found by the manager until Monday morning.

All in all it is a very pleasant trip and I would not see the world any other way.

It takes the manager some time to work out why this delivery has been returned, for by now our faces are almost obscured with destination labels, stamps, and "This Way Up" stickers. Moreover the outer layer of clingfilm is somewhat discolored by dust, oil, saltwater, and the effusions found at the bottom of whaling ships. We have been garlanded with flowers by hippies in San Francisco, swaying maidens in Hawaii and holy men in India as we floated down the River Ganges at one point. Eventually, however, he peels aside enough of the accumulated debris to recognize us.

"Also," he says. "This is somewhat irregular."

He summons flunkeys to release us. I cannot repress a wistful sigh of regret. Happily it takes them some time to unwrap us, as they cannot find the end of the clingfilm. Eventually we are released, perfectly preserved and as fresh as daisies. However, it is a while before we can use our limbs properly and for some time we have to be wheeled about on trolleys.

Soon our voyage is just a happy memory. It is never to fade or be forgotten, but time changes all things and no man can predict the vagaries of the future. Only loss and things wrapped in clingfilm are eternal.

And so we beat on, boats against the current, borne back ceaselessly into the past.

Chapter 50

It ends at the concert Roy Orbison is playing at the clingfilm factory. Happy workers shuffle their feet in time to the music and gaily wave streamers of clingfilm in the air as Roy regales them with his hits.

During the interval the mayor of Düsseldorf comes onstage and presents Roy and Jetta and I with medals for our diligence while the crowd applaud and nod their heads with approval. Then the manager gives us passes to the clingfilm factory so we can go there any time we want, even at night or during holidays, and rescinds the order that I am banished and cannot send him letters or smile at him through the windows of his house or clean his car or post chocolates and flowers and thank-you notes through his letterbox or put on women's clothing and wigs and attempt to talk to him in cocktail bars or sleep on his roof or lobby religious leaders for his canonization. I may now do all of these things if I want, or some of them anyway, but I do not wish to as it has already been explained to me that he did not invent clingfilm.

He further presents us with a lifetime's supply of clingfilm. I estimate that I already have one of those, but you cannot be too careful and besides I do not wish to seem ungrateful, so I merely smile and bow my thanks.

Finally the mayor gives Jetta a bucket of prime Pomeranian worms tied up with a little ribbon and the crowd says "Ah."

However, then a problem arises.

"*Ach*," says Roy backstage, "that pestilent jackal of the press and his intrusive ways! Behold this."

He passes me the latest edition of *Rolling Stone* magazine which a flunkey has just delivered.

On the front cover is a picture of Roy—wrapped up in clingfilm! It is an enlarged still from the footage taken by the film crew when Roy hopped past in the park.

"It is not your best side, Roy," I say, "but it captures your essential vigor and zeal."

"Wait until you read the article," admonishes Roy, moaning and wringing his hands.

Obediently I turn to the story within.

"NEW DIRECTION FOR ORBISON?" it is titled.

It continues:

"Also.

"I have to report that there is exciting news for music fans from the pleasant and orderly city of Düsseldorf. For Mr. Roy Orbison, that well-known rock troubadour and man in black, has been behaving in a singular fashion of late. At the climax of his recent concert in the city (at which, as a separate review will attest, not a wrong note was played) Orbison surprised and delighted his fans by playing an encore wrapped entirely in a clinging plastic-like material of wondrous translucence— later established by this reporter's diligence to be a miracle substance known as 'clingfilm,' said to be used in catering.

"Moreover Orbison, who is thought to hail from North America originally, has been delighting his show business friends by donning this strange attire at private soirees, and some of them intend to follow his lead.

"'It was groovy, man,' said Mr. James Morrison of the Doors. 'It was like some cosmic birth caul, and then he popped out. I want to take that trip.'

"While Mr. Morrison sadly admits that his brain cannot be relied upon for purposes of verification, both Yul Brynner, the noted bald actor, and Miss Mitzi Klavierstuhl, the acceptable face of weather-prediction, independently confirmed that it was so.

"At a park the next day Mr. Orbison was spotted energetically hopping along wrapped in the wonder substance in the company of his friend Mr. Ulrich Haarbürste and the latter's well-groomed terrapin, Jetta.

"What can this portend? Is it some witty statement of the barrier between artist and audience? An acknowledgment of the impermeable membrane that separates one individual mind from another through which all our attempts at communication are somewhat muffled? Could it be some defiant declaration that his music will never go stale? Is he symbolically donning the mantle of a prophet or savant of a coming new age of scientific marvel? Is it perhaps some high-tech shroud heralding a new techno-gothic direction to his music? Does Orbison adopt this garb simply for the interesting acoustic effect? Or to increase the air of mystery and enigma already fostered by his trademark dark glasses?

"Who can tell?

"But in this reporter's humble opinion it is the most exciting development in rock music since the wah-wah pedal.

"Orbison has proved himself a trailblazer and in consequence I await his new album with a keenness that falls just the right side of unseemly impatience. Meanwhile all rock fans, musicologists or interested observers of fashion are counseled to attend one of Orbison's shows as soon as they can fit it into their schedule to observe this fascinating new development for themselves. Intellectual stimulation and a more visceral enjoyment seem certain.

"PS!

"Another thought has just entered my brain. It occurs that no man can predict the future and I cannot in conscience guarantee that Orbison will repeat his experiment in future concerts. If he does not do so, I for one would be disappointed and in that case it could only be concluded that he is not a trailblazer after all but rather a whim-tossed gadfly who wore clingfilm in some deplorable bid for momentary attention."

"You perceive?" says Roy. "I am finished in this business."

"How so, Roy?"

"When I am not wrapped in clingfilm at this or any other concert I will be deemed a vapid dilettante and flibbertigibbet who has trifled with people's artistic expectations!"

I cough discreetly. "Of course, there is one thing we might try . . ."

Roy wrings his hands again. "I perceive what is in your mind but I could not ask. I could not possibly ask you to follow me wherever I go and attend every concert, show business soiree, and gala premiere and wrap me in clingfilm at the climax of each. Could I?" He looks pleading. "It would mean free tickets and backstage passes for you and Jetta for life."

"What are friends for, Roy?"

And so, ten minutes later . . .

Who could have predicted that I and my terrapin Jetta would again step onstage during Roy Orbison's concert, or that I would be given a contract to become one of his entourage and have to wrap him in clingfilm at every concert and social occasion for the rest of my life? Yet such is the thing that has occurred.

"Thank you, Düsseldorf," says Roy into the microphone after playing the second half of his set with pinpoint accuracy. "You have been a well-behaved audience. Yet I can tell there is something you have been waiting for and keenly anticipating . . . "

There are excited murmurs and the crowd nudge each other.

"You will not be disappointed! I hereby present my close friend Ulrich Haarbürste, a local man of exemplary diligence, and his terrapin Jetta!" There are cheers for both of us. "He will now completely wrap me in clingfilm!"

As the crowd cheers ecstatically, I take out my clingfilm and bow.

"Commence," says Roy.

I start from the feet and work my way up. I must work diligently and yet with a rock and roll attitude. It is strange yet wonderful to be wrapping him knowing that even if he is released I will soon be able to wrap him again, not once but many times. Soon, Roy Orbison is completely wrapped in clingfilm. My happy switch is set to the maximum.

I take the microphone. "You are completely wrapped in clingfilm!" I announce.

The crowd goes wild and so does my heart. Even Jetta seems strangely moved and later on does some stage diving.

Appendix

German-Language Tales

You may sometimes forget that, like Conrad and Nabokov, English is not my first language. Nevertheless such is the case.

Nowadays I write most of my tales of Roy in Clingfilm in English for a number of reasons. However, there exist several tales written in German which I have not translated, as certain nuances would be lost. As a curiosity I append three of them here so that you may compare.

Future scholars should note that these stories occur at various points in the timeline of the canon.

With that I bid you farewell. If you have enjoyed this book you should certainly recommend it to your friends, and perhaps indulge in discreet lobbying of the Nobel Prize committee.

—Ulrich

Auf Dem Strand

Ich liege neben dem Wasser mit meine Beinahe-Schildkröten-ähnlichen-Geschöpf heisst Jetta. Plötzlich kommt er entlang der Sand—Herr Roy Orbison, die berühmt Meistersinger.

Weil es ein sonniger Tag ist und wir sind am Strand, er ist gekleidet in ein schwarzes bade-anzug und zwei Paare von schwarze Augenglas, ein Paar über den anderen.

"Guten Nachmittag, Roy," Ich sage. "Was Machen Sie am Beach?"

"Ich wünsche Sonnenschein," sagt Roy.

"Eure Deutsch ist sehr gut."

"Dein auch."

Ich verbeuge.

"Achtung!" sagt einen Publik-Ansage Tannoy Laut-sprecher plötzlich. "Vorsichtig von Solar Radiazion! Nicht zu vergessen zu machen mit der Sonnenschein-Creme, oder ein schreckliche Schicksal wartet Sie!"

"Ach," sagt Roy, "Ich bin spurlos versenkt. Ich habe meine Sonnenschein-Creme vergessen!"

"Natürlich, ich würde meinen geben," Ich sage, "aber Ich habe es aller auf meiner Beinahe-Schildkröten-ähnlichen-Geschöpf geputtet. Aber Halt! Ich habe einen Kopf Sturm! Glücklicherweise habe ich ein Zylinder oder zwei, oder es ist möglich drei, von besitzensuchenzugenmachenübergruppenschnurpenplastische mit mir, für mannigfach ganz unschuldigen Gründe. Wenn ich Sie in dem besitzensuchenzugenmachenübergruppenschnurpenplastische mantel, es würde Sie von dem Solar-Radiazion schützen, aber Eingang erlauben zu der gesund Sonnenschein!"

"Wunderbar," sagt Roy. "Es ist klar. Sie müssen mich im besitzensuchenzugenmachenübergruppenschnurpenplastische bedecken, schnell."

Ich beginne an seinen Pflip-Pfloppen und arbeit meine Weg aufwärts. Ich wickele ihn schnell aber mit diligenz. Bald, Roy Orbison ist völlig gewickelt mit besitzensuchenzugenmachenübergruppenschnurpenplastische. Es ist Sonnenschein innen meine Herz.

"Sie sind ganz gewickelt im besitzensuchenzugenmachenübergruppenschnurpenplastische," Ich sage.

"Bitte," sagt Roy, "Employen Sie das intimat Du."

"Vielen Dank! Du bist ganz gewickelt im besitzensuchenzugenmachenübergruppenschnurpenplastische. Und du kannst 'Du' zu mir auch sagen."

"Vielleicht ein anderes Zeit."

Wir kommenzen zu sonnen-baden.

"Du kennst, es schlägt mir," Ich sage, gedankevoll, "dass Wenn man das Wort 'besitzensuchenzugenmachenübergruppenschnurpenplastische' abkürzen könnte, die Schachteln würden nicht haben wie lang zu sein."

"Der Kugelschreiber von meinen Onkel ist auf der Tisch von meine Tante," antwortet Roy, enigmatische.

Auf der Sprache Klasse

Diese zeit bin ich helfen Roy zu bürsten hinauf seine Deutsch, und wer besser als ich?

"Die Beinahe-Schildkröten-ähnlichen-Geschöpf (wer heisst Jetta) ist auf der Tisch von meinen Deutsch-Lehrer," Roy sagt, mit einem Punkt in Richtung zu Jetta, wer sicherlich ist auf meinen Tisch in ihrer Rolle von Klasse Monitor.

"Aber gut!" sagt ich. "Und wo ist das besitzensuchenzugenmachen-übergruppenschnurpenplastische?"

"Das besitzensuchenzugenmachenübergruppenschnurpenplastische von meinen Deutsch-Lehrer ist nächst zu die Beinahe-Schildkröten-ähnlichen-Geschöpf."

"Viel Besser! Aber deinen Akzent braucht arbeit."

"Akzent, pfui!" sagt Roy. "Wenn das Worten sind richtig, oder in dem richtige Ball-Park, die Akzent macht nichts."

Ich entscheide zu lehre Roy ein Lektion—nach alle, dass ist warum wir sind hier. . .

Roy erhebt seinen Hand in die Luft. "Erlaubnis zu gehen zu dem Bade-zimmer," er sagt.

Schnell, ich gegrabben das besitzensuchenzugenmachenüber-gruppenschnurpenplastische and wickeln er mit es. Ich arbeit mit Eile und Eifer damit er hat kein zeit zu protestieren. Bald, Roy Orbison ist ganz gewickelt mit besitzensuchenzugenmachenüber-gruppenschnurpenplastische. Jetzt ich bin der Schüler und Freude ist der Lehrer.

"Was gibt?" sagt Roy, ein bischen vermufflet.

"Du bist ganz gewickelt im besitzensuchenzugen-machenüber-gruppenschnurpenplastische," ich sage, "an deine wünsche."

"Meine wünsche?"

Ich falte die Stirn. "Hast Du nicht fragen mir? Du hast gesagt dass viele Motten wünsche zu essen deine warenzeichen schwarze Kleidung, und dass Ich sollte bedeckst du im besitzensuchenzugen-machenübergruppenschnurpenplastische schnell!"

"Ach," sagt Roy. "Ich gemeinte dass nicht. Ich suchte erlaubnis zu gehe zu dem kleine Jungen zimmer. Ich muss ein umlaut irgendwo verloren haben. Es scheint, dass Akzent *ist* wichtig, nach alle."

Jetta fällt von der Tisch, entweder wegen sie lacht sehr viel, oder wegen sie braucht augen-glases.

Die Unmoralischen Mädchen von Bavaria

Ich und meine kleine Beinahe-Schildkröten-ähnlichen-Geschöpf heisst Jetta sind auf Tour mit Roy Orbison. Wir haben Eingang-alle-Zonen Reisepässe und wir haben Erlaubnis zu essen drei komplimentarische zurück-Bühne Würsten pro Person.

Roy kommt zurück-Bühne nach dem Ende von seine Bavarische Konzert, dass sehr gut und effizient war.

"Jetzt für Ruhe und effizient Zimmerservice auf meinen Hotel," er Seufzer.

Aber wann er die Bühne Tür öffnet, viele Schreien kommen zu uns!

"Ach," er sagt, schliessen es schnell, "es gibt viele weiblich Pop-fanatiker und Musikkapellesexuellvorliebemädchen heraus dort! Sie enthalten Bavarische Milch-Mädchen und ähnliche Damen von elastischen moralische. Ich muss von diesen hysterisch Frauen umarmt und geküsst sein, aber ich fürchte mich, dass Ich von ihnen eine Küssend-Krankheit konnte fangen. Sie konnten auch meine warenzeichen schwarze Kleidung zerreissen für nicht-Lizenziert Andenken, und gegrabben meine Mannschlange ohne Erlaubnis."

Ich sage, "Es gibt ein Ding wir mögen versuchen. Ich könnte Du vielleicht aufwickeln in einen schützend Deckel von besitzensuchen-zugenmachenübergruppenschnurpenplastische."

"Ach gut," sagt Roy. "Dieses ist der Weg zu gehen. Kommenzen Sie schnell."

Ich starte von dem Fuss und arbeite meine weg zum Kopf. Ich arbeite vorsichtig damit keine Harpie können erreichen seinen Mannschlange. Bald, Roy Orbison ist ganz gewickelt mit besitzensuchenzugenmachenübergruppenschnurpenplastische. Der Hund von meine Freude springt über der Tisch von Ekstase.

"Du bist ganz gewickelt mit besitzensuchenzugenmachenüber-gruppenschnurpenplastische," Ich sage.

"Das Kapital."

Ich öffne die Tür und Roy springt durch die Allee. Die ventilator-frauen werfen sich an er und küssen und fassen er, aber das besitzensuchenzugenmachenübergruppenschnurpenplastische abschirmt ihn. Wir kommen in die Sicherheit der Limousine und fahren ab. Das besitzensuchenzugenmachenübergruppenschnurpenplastische ist mit dem küssen von Lippenstift bedeckt, aber Roy ist unbeschädigt.

"Die Strategie hatte Erfolg an allen Punkten," sagt Roy fröhlich.

"Ich bin so dankbar, dass ich Sie küssen könnte."

"Aber Roy," Ich sage, "Ich konnte etwas fangen!"

"Deine Mutti ist ein Tisch-Tänzer," lacht Roy.

About the Author

Ulrich Haarbürste lives quietly and tidily in Düsseldorf, Germany, with his terrapin. He has twice won a civic award for Most Orderly Flower Bed.

He has now retired from writing fiction as he had nothing left to achieve. However, he acts as mentor to a select group of aspiring writers, teaching an intensive course in punctuation, not writing in the margins, and correct posture. He also is involved in consumer activism, spending a lot of time comparing and contrasting different brands of a certain kitchen product. A monograph on this topic may be forthcoming.

Recently he made the news after being banned from a number of music venues, following an unusual incident with a hologram Roy Orbison. About this Haarbürste remains baffled and saddened and only wishes to say that if Roy has grown so grandiose as to refuse to perform in person he will soon lose touch with his fan base.